juniors

The Mystery at Poor Boy's Folly

Bernard Palmer

ACCENT BOOKS

Denver, Colorado

ACCENT BOOKS
A division of Accent Publications, Inc.
12100 W. Sixth Avenue
P.O. Box 15337
Denver, Colorado 80215

Copyright © 1981 Accent Publications, Inc.
Printed in the United States of America

Library of Congress Catalog Card Number: 80-65058

ISBN 0-89636-049-0

1

The wind swooped over the scraggly mountain ridge and rushed through the aspen forest along the slope that held the crumbling remains of what used to be Poor Boy's Folly. The hastily built town that had once roared with the rumble of wagons and the lusty shouts and laughter of the miners had long since fallen silent. The town had been given over to the squirrels, rabbits and birds who still claimed the mountain. Until that morning! It all started with the auction.

Cars, pickups and campers from as far away as Denver and Colorado Springs had made their way off the busy Interstate and up the steep, twisting road to the ghost town. By ten o'clock the narrow, rutted street that footed the abandoned stores and saloons, the rooming houses and towering three-story hotel was clogged with vehicles. The rotting boardwalk rang with the clatter of hard leather and for the first time in more years than he could remember Hubert Heskett, the owner and proprietor of the little general store and service station on the edge of the community, had more customers than he could handle.

Gangling, tow-headed, fourteen-year-old Greg Powell rested his hand on the new 35 mm camera suspended from a wide strap around his neck and looked about.

"Wow!" he exclaimed to his companions. "Dad was sure right when he said the auction today was going to be a blast!"

"You can say that again," his new friend, Hank Wendland, murmured. "There're more people than I've *ever* seen around here at one time."

Hipolita Rodriguez, Greg's pal from Concord, Colorado who had come to the mountains with the Powell family, was unimpressed. "That doesn't mean a thing," he blurted. "They've only come to buy junk."

"It is not junk," twelve-year-old Kim Powell informed him archly. "This is an antique sale."

"Antique—Schmantique! It's all the same to me—a big fat drag!"

"You just say that," Kim countered, "because you don't know how to appreciate beautiful things."

"It's still junk and I don't see why we've got to waste our time watching somebody sell it. We could go fishin' or hunting for old abandoned mines or—or *anything* else."

"Can't do it," Greg said. "Dad had to go to Denver this morning to meet with the editor about this book of photographs of old ghost towns that he's doing. He asked me to get some shots of the crowd for him."

"It sounds like *you're* stuck," Hip said, laughing. "But we aren't. Come on, Kim. Let's find something else to do."

"No way. I want to see what they've got for sale."

"I can answer that without even going inside. There'll be a bunch of old furniture and dishes, and broken clocks."

"I heard Dad and Mom talking about it last night," Hank put in. "They said that the people who own the mine and the ghost town have been keeping all the furniture and dishes and whatever they found in the buildings after everyone moved out—even the mining equipment—in a big Quonset hut behind Mr. Heskett's general store. It's been there for years and years, but now they've decided to sell all of it. That's why they're having this auction."

Hip was still disinterested. Greg didn't care much for looking at a bunch of old stuff either, but there was no getting out of it for him. Without answering his friend, he moved slowly forward in the direction of the door to the huge hotel lobby where the sale was to take place.

Greg and his friends were at the corner of the building when their attention was drawn to the slight, bent figure of a graying Oriental man. But the gaunt stranger held Greg's interest for only a moment. He was accompanied by a wee slant-eyed girl who looked to be a year or two younger than Kim. Her ebony hair was cut in bangs across her forehead and hung straight and neat about her ears. Her features were dainty and as exquisite as fine china, and her eyes were as black as her hair. Black and distressingly sad. A hint of tragedy marred her beautiful profile and she did not smile.

"Who's that?" Greg asked softly, turning to Hank.

"That's Wai Chun Hing. He's always lived here, I guess. My dad was born on the mountain and he said that Hing has been around for as long as he can remember. According to what everybody says, his dad was an important person around here."

"But . . . who's that with him?" Greg persisted. He had been vaguely curious about the elderly man but his real concern was for the girl. She was so very pretty and seemed so forlorn and depressed. "Who is she?"

Hank shrugged. "Search me. Nobody ever saw her around here until her family moved in near Wai Chun Hing's. I don't know where they were from. They certainly didn't look like the Orientals I've seen."

"They all look the same to me," Hip broke in.

"Anyway," Hank continued, "when they left, this girl must've stayed behind. That was the first any of us ever saw her with Wai Chun Hing, but now she's with him all the time."

Hip's eyes narrowed suspiciously. "Maybe he kidnapped her and is holding her for ransom."

"You've been watching too much TV," Greg snorted.

While they were talking in guarded tones the old man and his young companion paused momentarily before the hotel door. Then they shuffled inside.

"I still think he's holding her for ransom," Hip whispered, his voice taut with excitement.

"And I think you're off your nut," Greg replied.

"I think she's lonely," Kim said after a moment or two. "Did you see that look in her eyes? She's very sad."

Hip was not willing to concede defeat. "She looks that way because the old boy kidnapped her and she's afraid of what he'll do if she tries to run away."

"Pipe down, will you?" Greg demanded.

"OK. OK. But when you find out that I'm right, don't say I didn't warn you. I told you what was going on when we had a chance to do something about it, but you wouldn't listen to me."

Several people came up behind them and the youthful foursome moved from the doorway and stepped inside. They stopped momentarily, blinking in the subdued light. There was no electricity in the hotel and gas lamps were sputtering from various vantage points in the big room. In spite of their efforts, however, the room was still comparatively dark. The windows along either side of the lobby had been boarded up and the panes in front failed to let in enough of the sun's brilliance to chase away the gloom.

While Greg fumbled with his camera, a feeling of melancholy and foreboding swept over him. That Hip with his guarded whispers about kidnapping! He felt like kicking him!

Greg jerked his thoughts away from the little Oriental girl who had entered the hotel moments ahead of him and his companions. By this time his eyes were accustomed to the dull light and his attention was drawn to the tables arranged along the walls. They were massive, hand-carved pieces made of solid cherrywood, with chairs to match. The years of hard usage in the old mining town hadn't seemed to affect them more than to dull their varnished exterior.

Next to the tables and chairs stood two or three rows of solid oak or fruitwood bedroom suites, with beds, dressers and commodes to match. Long tables in the center of the big room were covered with smaller antiques.

At the front of the room in the center stood a small table with two chairs behind it; one for the clerk and one for his helper. To one side there was a lectern for the auctioneer. The rest of the room was filled with folding chairs so the buyers could be comfortable.

Greg's gaze picked up the slender figure of Wai Chun Hing and his petite young companion. They were moving slowly a dozen paces or so ahead of him and his friends. An aura of mystery surrounded the couple and Greg found himself pushing forward in an effort to get close enough to hear what they were saying to each other.

At the same time Hip reached over and poked Greg in the ribs. "Aren't you going to take any pictures?"

By this time the old man had returned an antique jade necklace to the table and moved stiffly forward. Greg couldn't imagine what such a piece of jewelry was doing in the hotel, except for the fact that the mine had used a lot of

Oriental workers in the old days and he supposed one of them could have left it in one of the rooms . . . or maybe it had been sold to someone in the hotel . . . or stolen. . . . Greg's youthful imagination conjured up several possibilities.

The youthful Chicano repeated his question, dragging Greg from his reverie. "Later," he said in disgust. "As soon as I see something good to take pictures of."

Turning his back on his friend, he studied the people ahead of him, trying to decide whom he should photograph. He wondered how his dad ever made up his mind on a worthy subject.

Greg didn't know when or how he came to notice the two men who were some distance ahead. Of medium build and nicely dressed, they appeared to be about the same age as his dad, or a little older. Soon Greg was close enough to hear what they were saying to each other, even though he was not trying to eavesdrop. Just two or three steps away, one of the men held an Oriental figurine in his hand. That, too, must have come from the Oriental section of Poor Boy's Folly.

"Did you see that old chink's eyes light up when he saw this piece, C. J.?"

"So?"

"Maybe we ought to bid on it."

"That," the one called C. J. said firmly, "is stupid."

His companion pulled in a deep breath and leaned forward to whisper something. His voice was so low Greg couldn't be sure of what he said, but he thought the stranger had made a remark about the old ghost town being the answer to their problem.

C. J. straightened and turned deliberately. Greg realized that the man was trying to make it appear as though he was unconcerned about what was going on around them, but Greg had the uneasy feeling that the hawk-faced stranger was keenly aware of everything that was taking place. And, more important, he was determined to find out if anyone had been listening to him and his companion. After surveying all the people close to the two, he at last seemed satisfied that no one had placed any significance in their conversation.

He turned back to his friend and spoke again. "We've got to be positive, Monte," he murmured. "I'm like you. I think it'll do fine, but we can't make a mistake."

At that moment the auction clerk approached the two men. "That's a beautiful figurine, isn't it?" he asked.

C. J. was startled. "What figurine?"

"The piece you have in your hand."

"Oh—Oh." C. J. seemed genuinely embarrassed. "I'm sorry. I picked it up to look at it and my friend called my attention to some of these other beautiful antiques. I was so carried away that I completely forgot I was holding the figurine."

"That's quite all right." The clerk took the piece from him and returned it to the table.

While this was going on Hip punched Greg in the ribs again and motioned to his camera, then at the two men. Greg nodded and backed away a couple of steps, focusing the camera deliberately. The men were so engrossed in their conversation with the clerk they didn't notice that Greg was even using his camera until the flash exploded.

The man called Monte jerked frantically at the sudden light and for an instant fear mingled with the anger in his eyes.

"You—" he snarled, savagely.

But C. J. laid a restraining hand on his arm. "Easy," he whispered in warning.

"Easy? You know what—"

"Please excuse my friend," C. J. said amiably. "He dislikes having his picture taken."

By this time the boys and the two strangers had attracted the attention of almost everyone around them.

"We're disturbing the people," C. J. continued, his voice quiet and friendly. "Let's go outside and talk, shall we?"

"But—" Greg started to protest that they had nothing to talk about, but the tall, moustached individual took him by the arm and started for the hotel door. Monte and the other kids followed.

Once they were outside, Greg was sure that C. J. and his friend were going to pounce on them about the picture, but they did not. Monte looked as though he wanted to, but it was obvious that his companion was firmly in charge.

C. J.'s smile broadened as he saw that Greg's camera was new. "I'll bet you got that for your birthday," he said.

The boy shook his head. "I bought it with the money I earned helping Dad."

"Good boy." He reached over and touched the camera with his forefinger. "I've always been interested in cameras. Is it OK if I look at it?"

Reluctantly Greg slipped the strap over his head and handed the camera to the stranger. He didn't want to but he could think of no good reason for refusing. Besides, there was something compelling about C. J. He seemed to be used to getting his way.

"This is the sort of camera I'd like," the man went on. As he spoke he fingered it casually. "I—" He pressed the release and the camera back snapped open, ruining the film.

"Hey!" Greg grabbed for his camera.

C. J. released it to him. "I'm sorry," he said, contrite and apologetic. "I—" He rummaged for his billfold. "Here's five dollars. That ought to pay for the roll of film, hadn't it?"

"Yes, but—"

"Sorry it happened. Buy yourself a roll of film and treat your friends to some pop or ice cream with what's left over. OK?"

Greg stared after C. J. and Monte as they turned and went back to the hotel. For a minute neither Greg nor his companions spoke.

"That dirty rat!" Hank exclaimed at last. "He did that on purpose!"

Greg nodded.

"Now," Hip exclaimed triumphantly, "maybe you'll listen to me when I say something weird's goin' on around here."

"You were talking about Wai Chun Hing and the girl," Hank reminded him.

"That was before I saw those two characters. They're in this with Wai Chun Hing."

"No way," Greg retorted.

"It's got to be something like that," Hip continued. "Those guys had some very good reason for not wanting their pictures taken."

Greg had to agree with that. It hadn't been an accident that C. J. had opened the back of the camera, ruining the film.

"Let's go down and get another roll of film," Hip said. "If we hurry, we can get back before they leave and get another picture of them."

"No. No!" Kim exclaimed quickly, fear rising in her voice. "Just looking at those two men gives me the shivers!"

2

There had been great excitement at the Powell home in Concord, Colorado that spring before the family and Hipolita Rodriquez went to the old ghost town where George Powell would be working on a photographic assignment. The newspaper Mr. Powell worked for had been sold to a syndicate from Denver and Mr. Mueller, the owner and publisher, was retiring. The family was sitting around the table after devotions one evening when Mr. Powell made the announcement of the sale.

Mrs. Powell gasped her surprise.

"What does that mean, Dad?" Kim wanted to know. "About you, I mean."

"The new owners have asked me if I would take over as editor."

Ten-year-old Kevin sighed his relief. "Then there's no sweat about you losing your job."

"Only it's not quite as simple as that, Kevin," their dad said.

Greg felt a chill sweep over him. It sounded as though his dad was going to tell them that he had decided to take a job somewhere else, a job that would make them have to move from Concord. "What do you mean?" he asked.

"I didn't quite have the confidence to go into business for myself as a freelance photographer," he explained, "until I got the assignment to do that picture story on the Little Mavericks' Rodeo for *Western World* and got some nice comments from a few readers. They have given me the encouragement I need to try it on my own."

"Hey, that's neat!" Greg exclaimed. "We won't have to move." And then he realized that a change of location could be entirely possible. "Or, will we?"

Mr. Powell looked from one to the other. "What do the rest of you want to do? Move somewhere else or stay here?"

Their voices were a chorus. "Stay!"

His grin revealed that he felt the same way. "Then I see no reason for moving."

In spite of the fact that they were going to be staying in Concord, Greg was concerned about the change in his dad's job. He knew that there would be few assignments in the immediate area and he was afraid that photography would take his dad away from home so much they would never get to see him.

That was not the way it had worked out, however. George Powell had a big assignment waiting. He was going to do a picture book on ghost towns of the Rockies, a job that would mean moving around quite a bit, so he bought a motor home and took his family along for the summer.

As soon as school was out he had hitched their pickup behind the new motor home, loaded his family and Greg's best friend Hip into it, and they had all come to Poor Boy's Folly where Mr. Powell started to work.

At first Greg had been afraid that he and Hip would be separated for the summer. That was the only thing he didn't like about the plan. He and his Chicano friend hadn't been parted for more than a few days at a time since Greg had moved to Concord three years before. He couldn't imagine having any real fun without Hip around. They were together constantly—in school and out.

When the decision was made to travel to the mountains that summer Greg resigned himself to being away from his friend, but that was before his dad asked if he would like to take Hip along.

"Do you mean it?" he asked, his eyes widening.

"I was talking with Mr. Rodriquez this morning," George Powell said. "He's given his permission."

"That's a piece of cake!" Greg exclaimed.

So, when the motor home had pulled out of Concord Hip was with the Powells and the kids' horses were at the Lazy H Ranch where Frank Ellis would take care of them.

Originally Mr. Powell had planned on staying in one location a couple of weeks before moving on to the next. However, they liked the area around Poor Boy's Folly so well Mr. Powell decided to let the family remain there while he drove to the other locations.

The kids thought they would be camping in a lonely place where they would have to depend on being with each other for entertainment, but they were surprised to find that a number of families lived on the slope near the deserted mining town.

There was a forest ranger and his family, and Hubert Heskett who owned and operated the general store and service station on the edge of the ghost town, the man who ran the road grader and two or three small ranchers, in addition to a number of others they had heard about but hadn't met yet.

"Think you'll like it here?" Mr. Powell had asked his family at the supper table several nights after they had found a suitable camping spot and settled in.

"Like it?" Greg echoed. "It's goin' to be great. Isn't it, Hip?"

"Far out."

"There is something that really disturbs me, though," Mrs. Powell put in. "I was talking to a woman who lives up the road a ways. She was telling me that there's no Sunday school or church anywhere around here."

Kim's eyes widened.

"I could hardly believe it myself," Mrs. Powell said, spreading a thin film of honey on her bread. "I honestly didn't think there was any place in Colorado where there wasn't at least *one* Sunday school. I've been sick about it ever since I talked with Mrs. Wendland."

"Mrs. Wendland?" Greg echoed. "We met her son, I'll bet. His name's Hank, and Hip and I got acquainted with him yesterday."

"She said she had a boy but she didn't say what his name was. Or, if she did, I missed it. I was so disturbed about what she told me I might not even have heard his name."

"It must be rough," Greg put in. He was thinking about their new friend and wondering what
it would be like to have been born and raised
in a place where he would have had no chance
of learning about Jesus. For as long as Greg
could remember, his family had been in Sunday
school and had taken an active part in the
services of the church. It had been so much a
part of his life that he hadn't even wondered
what it would be like not to be able to go to
Sunday school. And the worst of it was that
most people like Hank and his family would
probably not even know what they were
missing.

For a time silence held the little group in its
iron fist. The radio gave the time and weather,
but no one was listening.

"Dad," Kevin said at last. "Isn't there something we could do about it—while we're here, I
mean?"

Mrs. Powell's face brightened. "I was thinking
the same thing. We could start a little Sunday
school right here in the motor home. I can talk
to Hank's mother in the morning. She'll probably be able to give us a list of the kids who live
close enough to be good prospects."

"And we can start visiting them right away
to invite them to our Sunday school," Kevin
said.

Ordinarily Greg didn't think much of his
younger brother's ideas, but he had to admit
this one was OK. Besides, he and Hip had been
wanting to get to know Arden and Scott. Hank

had been telling them what great guys they were.

Early the next morning Greg and Hip went over to see the Wendland boy while Kim and Kevin went in the opposite direction. They were going to stop by the Hayes' place and invite their daughter, Sandi. Then they were going up the mountain to the tower where the forest ranger worked and lived. He had two kids about Kevin's age, or a little older, who would be good prospects for the Sunday school.

Greg and his pal had been sure Hank would be excited about the possibility of having Sunday school for a few weeks, and were disappointed when he didn't show much interest. "It sounds like a drag to me," he said. "We have to be in school all week, nine months of the year. I can't see goin' back on Sunday during the summer."

The boys tried to tell their new friend that it wasn't boring but they did not succeed very well. Hank was unimpressed and said so. Finally, with some reluctance, he agreed to try it for a week or two. "But I'm tellin' you both right now," he said, "if I don't like it, I won't be comin' any more."

"Fair enough," Hip said quickly.

Greg and Hip had planned on getting Hank to go with them to talk to Arden and Scott, but they hadn't been prepared for his antagonism. Now they were afraid to take him along for fear he would say something that might turn off the other two. So they decided they would have to visit the Nitler and Merrill places alone.

That night at devotions Kevin and Kim had much to relate to the family and Hipolita. Sandi Hayes and her family had moved into the area from Pueblo a few weeks before. She had gone to Sunday school there and missed it dreadfully.

"You should've been there!" Kevin exclaimed. "She was so happy I thought she was going to cry."

Next, Greg and Hip told the family about their disappointing experience with Hank Wendland. "So," the Powell boy concluded, "we decided to go over and see the other guys alone."

"Sounds like a good idea," his dad replied. "At least until we get things moving and they have a chance to see what Sunday school is like."

Greg's plan was to see Arden Nitler and Scott Merrill the following morning, but that was before he remembered the auction and the fact that his dad had asked him to go over and take some pictures of the crowd, since Mr. Powell couldn't go himself. Greg didn't deceive himself that he would take anything good enough to use—unless he got lucky—but it was always a possibility.

The kids went to the old hotel the following morning. Instead of getting pictures of the crowd, however, Greg had gotten mixed up with those two ugly strangers. C. J. had outfoxed him by pretending to be interested in his camera and then opening the back and ruining the exposed film. In spite of the fact that C. J. had apologized and given him five dollars to pay for the roll, Greg knew it had all been an act to ruin the film.

With growing uneasiness he and his friends went down to the general store where they bought a new roll of film and some candy and returned to the hotel just in time for the auction to begin. C. J. and Monte were inside, sitting half a dozen rows or so ahead of the kids.

Greg tried to focus his attention on the auction, but his thoughts kept drifting to the two strangers. They seemed attentive enough to what was going on—as attentive as anyone else in the big crowd—but there was something about them that set them apart, that made them different and ominous. There was a quick furtive look in their eyes as they swept the entire room in front of them with cold stares. This sent shivers up Greg's spine.

The two men bid now and then, chiefly on Oriental objects offered for sale, but didn't seem to want to buy anything. At least, they always dropped out as soon as the auctioning became spirited.

Long before the last items were sold, Hip and Kevin had tired and wanted to leave. "Can't we get out of here?" Hipolita whispered.

Greg shook his head. "It's about over."

"It's been over for two hours as far as I'm concerned," Hip grumbled.

Several people sitting nearby turned to glare at Greg and Hip. The auctioneer stopped the sale and fixed his gaze steadily on the noisy culprits. In that moment, Hip and Kevin got to their feet and started out. Reluctantly Greg and Hank followed. Only Kim, flushing scarlet with embarrassment, remained.

"Well, now you've done it," Greg said in disgust when they were outside again. 'You fixed it so we had to leave or get kicked out."

"And just about in time, too," Hip told him, glancing at Kevin for support. "If I'd stayed in there any longer I'd have died right on the spot."

"Me, too."

Greg shook his head. There were times when he got so disgusted with those two he didn't even want to own up to the fact that he knew them. But he had other things on his mind, too. Things like that slick-talking C. J. and his friend, Monte.

"How long do you think *they'll* hang around?" he asked, changing the subject.

Hip pulled in a thin breath and turned to stare at the open door. Greg knew he half expected to see C. J. and Monte come storming outside looking for them.

"Search me," he said. "Why?"

"I just hope they stay inside for awhile, that's all."

"Now what're you cookin' up?" Hip demanded uneasily.

"Nothing much."

"Don't try to give us that malarky. It sounds like a real bummer to me—whatever it is."

"All I want to do is go over and take a squint at that car of theirs."

22

"Not me," his younger brother protested. "That's a good way to get our heads bashed in."

"There's no law against looking at a car," Greg said.

"Maybe not, but try to tell them that." Kevin's trembling voice faded into silence as he heard the heavy sound of men's boots behind them. "Don't look now," he managed, "but I think we're already in big trouble."

Greg turned, as though to look up the steep slope that towered above them to the west. His heart faltered and moisture gleamed on his forehead. C. J. and Monte had left the hotel and were coming toward them at a brisk pace.

3

Kevin Powell acted as though he was about to bolt and run but Greg grasped him quickly by the arm. "Hang loose," he whispered.

"What makes you think they're not so suspicious already that they'll grab us when they get close?" the younger boy demanded.

"They can't grab all of us," Hank said. "There's four of us. There's only two of them."

"I'm the littlest," Kevin continued. "I'm the first one they'll nab!"

"They're not going to do anything to us out here in the open in the middle of the day," Greg said scornfully.

"You hope!" Kevin muttered under his breath.

By this time the men were drawing close to the foursome. They paused within a dozen feet or so. "Hi," C. J. said, as pleasantly as though they were close friends. "Get tired of the auction?"

"I—I guess so," Greg muttered lamely.

"Can't say that I blame you," the gangly stranger went on. "I find auctions a terrible bore myself."

That was more than Hip could stand. "Then how does it happen that you came all the way up here to an auction?" he asked.

C. J.'s lower lip sagged and color crept into his lean cheeks. His eyes flashed and for an instant he did not speak.

"Yeah, C. J.," Monte broke in, laughing, as they walked toward their car. "If you find auctions such a drag, how come you hauled me all the way out here from Denver to go to this one?"

"Shut up and get in the car!" C. J. growled.

The rest of their conversation was drowned by the sound of the motor.

Greg saw that his younger brother was visibly relieved as the men drove past them down the road that went by the general store. It disappeared around the curve in the direction of the highway that led to Denver. Although he would not have admitted it, he was pleased as well.

"That's a relief," Kevin said aloud.

Hank Wendland nodded. "Those two are weird!"

"Come on," Greg ordered brusquely. "We've got things to do."

Still, Hipolita did not move. "There is something weird about those guys. Monte said that C. J. was interested in antiques, but they only bid on three or four things and didn't buy one."

"Neither did we," Hank reminded him.

"We didn't plan to."

"Maybe they didn't see anything they liked," Greg suggested.

"Could be, but C. J. was sure examining those Oriental pieces before the auction started. I think the clerk was afraid he was going to walk off with that figurine. If you ask me, he was mighty interested."

"Well," Greg said, shrugging, "whatever they planned on buying, they're gone now and we'll probably never see them again."

"That sure won't make me feel bad," Hip added.

The foursome went up the steep slope above the ghost town and spent the rest of the afternoon poking around the abandoned Poor Boy's Mine. The narrow gauge track, crusted with rust after decades of disuse, still led into the shaft that plunged into the darkness of the mountain's innards.

A small ore car stood alone just inside the mine opening and several others were scattered about the clearing, as though the men who had worked with them had been too tired when they left to put them away. An ore wagon stood along the wall of the cliff, just off of what was once a well-traveled road that led to the smelter a mile or so away. The tired remains of the old bunkhouse sagged wearily in the middle, like a swayback horse that had lived beyond its time.

"Wouldn't it have been neat to have lived here when the mine was working?" Kevin asked. "All that gold! Wow!"

"Gold?" Hank echoed scornfully.

"The gold they dug out of the mine."

"They didn't dig any gold out of here. This is a silver mine."

The sun had dropped behind the mountain range and darkness was stealing across the aspen-covered slope by the time Greg and his companions passed through the ghost town on their way back to the motor home. They were only a few paces above the graveled road when they heard a car coming. It was still some distance away, but the soft, rhythmic purring of the well-tuned engine drifted up to them.

"Sounds as though we're going to have company," Hip said apprehensively.

"It has to be someone who lives around here," Greg replied.

Hank Wendland listened for a moment. "That car doesn't belong to anyone who lives here."

"How do you know that?" Kevin asked scornfully.

"After you've lived here awhile you'll learn to recognize who's driving by the sound of the vehicle. My folks have a pickup, the Nitlers have a four-wheel drive and Sandi Hayes' dad has an old eight-cylinder Ford that makes more noise than the grader."

He laughed. "Yep, you'll soon be able to tell who's coming just by the sound of the engine."

"Then who's coming now?" Kevin insisted.

Hank shook his head. "I don't think I've *ever* heard that motor before."

Hip quickened his pace. "Let's get close enough to the road to see who it is. OK?"

As the car came into view the younger boy grabbed Hip by the arm and jerked him back. "Get down!" he whispered tautly. At that instant the headlights probed the brush over their heads as the vehicle swept past and was gone.

"Man!" Hip exclaimed. "That was close."

"What was that all about?" Greg asked, getting to his feet and brushing his jeans with his hands.

"Didn't you recognize that car?" his pal asked. "It was C. J. and Monte."

"You're putting me on."

"I caught a glimpse of it as it came around the corner just now."

"Against those headlights?" Greg sounded doubtful.

"It isn't all that dark yet," Hip said.

"I saw it, too," Hank put in.

"And so'd I," Kevin said, shivering fearfully. "It was theirs, all right. I'd recognize that car anywhere."

Greg felt the corners of his mouth tighten. "I thought those guys had headed back to Denver. That's what they said when they left us."

"That's what they wanted us to think," Hip replied.

Greg pushed his cap back and scratched his ear. "But why?" he asked of no one in particular.

Hip lowered his voice to a whisper. "I don't know," he said, "but whatever the reason, you can bet that it's a good one. They don't want anyone to know about it . . . They don't even want anyone to know that they're back here."

Kevin took a step or two downhill in the direction of the motor home. "I don't like being up here. It gives me the creeps."

Greg stepped out into the middle of the road and stared after the car that was now a dark, formless shape in the growing gloom.

"Did you notice?" he asked. "They're headed back to the ghost town."

"But why?" Hank asked uneasily. "There's nothing but a bunch of old empty buildings up there."

"Maybe they forgot something," Kevin said, "and came back for it."

"Maybe," his older brother acknowledged. "But if they forgot something, why would they wait until it was almost dark to come back for it. No, there's got to be some other reason for this visit. And, whatever it is, it isn't good . . . Not with a pair of dudes like them!"

"The only reason they'd sneak back," Hip observed, "would be to steal something."

"But there's nothing up there to steal," Hank broke in disdainfully. "Everything that was any good was taken out of the buildings years ago and stored in that Quonset behind Mr. Heskett's place."

"Maybe there are some things they missed," Greg said. He didn't see how that could be true, yet there had to be some reason for C. J. and Monte to come back to the ghost town.

"How about going back up there?" Hip suggested. "Those guys didn't see us so they wouldn't know we're onto them. They won't be suspecting a thing."

Kevin caught his breath. "Are you out of your mind? They'd be on us like an eagle on a rabbit before we knew it."

"Not if we just sneaked in close enough to see where they are," Greg continued. Now that he thought about it, he began to get excited. Maybe they could find out something about the mystery of those two strangers. "It would give us a clue as to where to look tomorrow when we're sure those guys are gone."

"No way," Kevin said firmly. "I'm going home."

"You can't do that!" his older brother retorted. "The folks'll wonder where Hip and I are and what we're doing."

In spite of his protests, Kevin joined the other three as they walked up the narrow, winding road. They kept close to the aspen-choked ditch so they could duck out of sight at the first sound of another vehicle coming from either direction.

Greg had been in favor of visiting the ghost town again in an effort to find out what C. J. and Monte were up to, but now that they were actually on their way, doubt swept over him. He could see the ominous, leering features of the two men in every tree and every turn in the trail.

What if they had actually seen him and his companions, and were hiding in the brush waiting to see if they would come along? What if they stumbled onto the strangers in the dark and got caught?

There were no police in the deserted ghost town. There weren't even any other adults, except old Hubert Heskett who didn't hear very well and was so crippled and arthritic he had difficulty even filling a car with gas. If the boys did blunder into C. J. and Monte, there would be no one to help them.

Greg paused momentarily. Maybe they were making a mistake. Maybe they should do like Kevin wanted and turn back.

"What's wrong?" Hank asked in a hoarse whisper. "See anything?"

Greg shook his head and moved forward once more, a bit slower this time. They were still a hundred yards from the faded sign that proclaimed the boundary of Poor Boy's Folly when Hank stopped, grabbing Greg and Hip by the arms.

"What is it?" Hip cried in a taut whisper.

"Look!"

"I'm looking. I'm looking."

"Not up the road! Where I'm pointing!"

They turned to their right and saw, not a dozen feet from them, the rear bumper of C. J.'s car. The vehicle had been pulled off the road and hidden so well it was all but impossible to see.

"I'm getting out of here!" Kevin exclaimed, stepping backward a pace or two.

"That's the best news I've heard all night!" Hip told him.

This time Greg and Hank did not protest. They knew that the two men were somewhere ahead—on foot. And in the growing darkness they might not even see them until it was too late. They turned and ran to catch up with their two companions, and it was two or three minutes before anyone spoke.

"That settles it," Greg said at last. "We know now that those characters are up to something."

"And whatever it is," Hank murmured, "I'll bet it's against the law."

"That means," Hip put in, "that it's dangerous for us to go poking around their car or in the ghost town when we have any idea they're around."

Greg did not answer, but he had to agree with Hip. It could be dangerous. There was the likelihood that C. J. and Monte wouldn't have any scruples against playing rough if they caught anyone meddling in their affairs. Yet, he couldn't help wondering what was going on.

Maybe, he thought, if he and his friends did just a little digging they could get to the bottom of the mystery. If they did, of course, they would have to be very careful to keep C. J. and Monte from knowing what they were doing or they would be in real trouble.

4

That night Hank stayed for supper with the Powells and Hipolita Rodriguez. At the time Greg had invited Hank he wasn't thinking about their evening devotions. Now he was beginning to wish he hadn't asked Hank over.

It would have been all right if Hank hadn't come on so strong against anything Christian. He didn't know much about the Bible and acted as though he didn't want to. Questions had gleamed in his eyes when they asked the blessing before the meal and again when Mr. Powell reached for the Bible after they ate.

"What're you goin' to do?" he blurted.

"We're reading from the second chapter of Titus tonight," George explained. "Then we'll have a time of prayer. We will be asking God to help us with the new Sunday school we're starting."

Hank sighed his resignation and leaned back in the chair to wait until they had finished.

"Do you always do this?" he asked.

"That's right," Greg answered.

Hank's lips curled in disgust. "What a drag!"

Greg felt like telling him not to knock it until he'd tried it, but changed his mind and said nothing.

The next morning Greg left the motor home with Hip and Kim shortly after breakfast and they made their way up the hill in the direction of the Nitler and Merrill homes. Both boys were home and sounded as though they were anxious to come to Sunday school, which was encouraging to Greg and his companions.

"Now where?" Kim asked as they left the Nitler yard.

"We could go back to Poor Boy's Folly and look for C. J. and Monte," Greg said, glancing impudently at his sister. "How does that grab you?"

"Not good," she retorted. "You can do what you want to but Hip and I aren't stupid enough to poke into that mess." She quickened her pace slightly.

"It sounds OK to me," Hip put in, disagreeing with Kim.

Greg shrugged. He hadn't really wanted to go back to the ghost town that morning anyway. He was still as curious as ever about the two men but they had some more kids to invite to Sunday school. Besides, he wasn't sure he wanted to be nosing around those buildings when there was a chance of running into those dudes.

"Who's next on the list?" he asked, changing the subject.

Kim stopped momentarily, her attractive young features serious. "I've been thinking about that little girl who was with old Wai Chun Hing at the auction," she said. "She looked so lonely. I'd like to invite her."

Hip's dark eyes were fixed on Greg's sister. "You can't mean that!"

"Why not? She needs Jesus, too."

"I know! But that old Oriental! He'll boil us in oil if he catches us! I'm not goin' near her."

"I'm not afraid of her," Kim retorted.

"Neither am I," Hip continued, "but did you see the way that old buzzard looked at us? It gave me the jitters."

Kim was unconvinced. "I still think we ought to go over and invite that girl to Sunday school tomorrow!"

"It won't do any good," Greg said. "Wai Chun Hing wouldn't let her come."

"I don't even want to go over there," Hip said. "When we're not watching he might zap us with a karate chop."

"If you two are afraid to go," Kim said, "I'll go alone."

"OK," Greg answered reluctantly. "We'll go along, but don't say we didn't warn you."

They went down the steep mountainside, across the road and angled diagonally through the forest. They jumped over a narrow icy stream and skirted a towering cliff to get to the place where the elderly, gray-haired Oriental man lived with the girl.

Greg paused briefly as they drew close enough to see the house through the trees. The building was small and neatly painted with a flower box on the window sill at either side of the door. The tiny yard was closely clipped and as clean as any park. Not a twig or a leaf or a scrap of paper could be seen anywhere.

"Well," Greg said, his voice hushed. "This is the place."

"I still think he kidnapped her and is holding her for ransom," Hip whispered.

They hesitated uneasily. Then Kim squared her shoulders and started forward. "Come on."

Her brother and his friend followed. They were crossing the lawn when the almond-eyed little girl came around the corner of the house, her gaze fixed on Kim.

"Hi," Kim said cordially.

The girl smiled nervously but did not reply.

"My name's Kim. What's yours?"

"Somi."

"Somi? I've never heard that name before. It's beautiful."

The girl's smile winked at Kim. "Thank you."

"You have such a pretty yard."

Somi's face darkened slightly. "I only live here for a little while," she said.

"We're only here for a little while, too, but we have decided to have Sunday school in our motor home for a few weeks. Would you like to come?"

Her tiny face scowled. "What's Sunday school?"

"All the kids around here are coming over to our place at 10 o'clock Sunday morning—that's tomorrow," she explained. "We'll be singing songs and reading the Bible and praying . . ."

Somi didn't seem to understand. "I—" she began questioningly.

At that instant the door opened and Wai Chun Hing appeared, his solemn face hard with emotion. "Somi!" he called loudly.

"Yes, Grandfather."

"Come here!... Now!" His voice was stern and imperious.

She started to leave but came back to Kim briefly, as though she couldn't bring herself to leave right then. "I—I'm sorry," she stammered. "I—"

The elderly man held the screen door open for her. A step or two from the house she paused, glanced hurriedly over her shoulder and disappeared inside. The door closed emphatically behind her.

For the space of a minute Kim was motionless, frozen by the sudden chill of the old man's behavior.

"Let's get movin'!" Hip urged, glancing uneasily about. "That old duffer's apt to come charging out of there anytime."

Kim was still not ready to leave. "Do you suppose it would do any good if I knocked on the door and tried to talk to him myself?" she asked. "Somi really wants to come to our Sunday school."

"But he's not going to let her," Greg replied.

"It isn't fair for him to treat her that way. She's got to have friends and he ought to let her go to Sunday school if she wants to."

"*Now* are you going to believe me when I tell you that Wai Chun Hing kidnapped her? Didn't you see how scared she is of him?"

"She didn't sound scared to me," Kim answered. "She called him 'grandfather.'"

"He'd probably beat her if she didn't," Hip persisted.

"I'd like to tell him some things!" Kim retorted sternly. "It's wrong for him to keep her away from other kids."

"Maybe so," her brother said, "but there's nothing we can do to change it, so we'd just as well forget about her."

"No way." Kim's jaw was set and fire gleamed in her eyes. Greg knew that she hadn't finished with Wai Chun Hing and the little girl he was taking care of.

"There's a mystery about C. J. and Monte and why they're fooling around up here," Hip said when they were halfway home, "but there's a mystery about Somi and the old man she calls 'grandfather,' too. Why do you suppose she's living there?"

"Maybe he is really her grandfather," Kim suggested.

He shook his head. "Hank says that they're no relation."

Greg listened thoughtfully. There *was* something of a mystery about the beautiful little Oriental girl and the old man.

When they got back to the motor home Hank Wendland was there, sitting at the table with a glass of milk and a plate of cookies in front of him. "I've been looking all over for you guys," he said.

Hip laughed. "I can see that."

They all had some cookies and milk and were outside before Hank told them the purpose of his visit.

"I was talking to my folks about the old ghost town this morning," he said softly. "They told me some stuff that was real interesting. They said there used to be a lot of robberies while the mines were operating. Two or three times a year thieves would knock off the silver bars that were being hauled from the smelter to Denver."

Hip crinkled his nose curiously. "What does that have to do with us?"

"Nothing." By this time Hank was whispering. "But it might have a lot to do with C. J. and Monte. We've been trying to figure out why they're hanging around up here. This could be the reason."

"Hey, that's right," Greg said. "They may think some of that stolen silver is hidden right in Poor Boy's Folly."

The kids stared at one another, the color fading from their cheeks. A person wouldn't think any of that silver would still be in the ghost town, Greg decided. It had been stolen such a long time ago, it was sure to have been carted away and spent. Yet, there had to be some reason for those two men to keep coming back to the ghost town.

"Do you really think that's what they're after?" Hip asked nervously.

"Could be," Greg said thoughtfully. "I've got an idea!"

"What's that?"

He put a finger to his lips as a warning for silence and went to the motor home door where he called out to his mother, "When will Dad be back?"

"Late this afternoon. Why?"

"Do you suppose it will be all right with him if we look through his research material?"

She came to the door, broom in hand. "I'm sure he wouldn't mind," she answered, "if you're careful not to destroy anything or get it out of sequence."

As soon as she finished sweeping she got the folder that contained the material her husband had gathered on Poor Boy's Folly and the mine that had given the ghost town its name.

"Now," Hank asked when they were once more alone, "what do you expect to find in a stack of old newspaper clippings?"

"Maybe nothing," Greg said, picking up a few yellowed news accounts of life in the roaring mining town.

"Then why are we doing this?" Hip asked in disgust.

"We just might find out something that would give us a clue as to what C. J. and Monte are after."

The kids divided the material into a pile for each and started to read. Most of the clippings were dull and uninteresting. There was a story from the *Denver Post* about a man who was trying to raise money to turn the old ghost town into a dude ranch. Another account spoke of a rumor that a highway was to be cut through the area, necessitating the destruction of the town and the Colorado Historical Society was alarmed. A third told of a rumored reopening of the Poor Boy Mine. A new find of silver was supposed to have been made that was large enough to warrant an extensive mining operation.

"Listen to this," Greg said, reading the account aloud.

His new friend laughed. "Dad told us about that," Hank said. "It's one of his favorite stories. People got all excited about the new vein of ore, but when they got the assayers' report there wasn't enough silver in it to pay the mining costs if the men had worked free."

They read on, growing more discouraged by the minute.

Kim had an article about the part the Chinese played in the operation of the mine and the large Oriental population in Poor Boy's Folly at the height of the silver rush. Because of her interest in Somi, she read it aloud.

"Hey," Hip said when she had finished. "I didn't know that any of the Orientals who worked up here were rich."

"A few were," Kim replied. "This story says that they went prospecting on their own and struck it rich."

Hank knew a little about that, too. His dad couldn't remember their names, he said, but he had told his family about the big Oriental house that stood on a bluff by itself. "Dad used to be afraid of it when he was a little kid," Hank laughed.

"What happened to it?" Greg wanted to know.

"It was burned down when Dad was a boy. And soon after that the Oriental families left. Nobody knows where."

The kids returned to their reading. They had almost finished when Greg found the sort of clipping he had been looking for.

"Listen to this!" he exclaimed. "'Two men believed to be part of the gang of desperadoes who held up the silver wagon hauling from the Poor Boy Smelter last month were apprehended in a Denver hotel. The silver was not in their room and intensive questioning has failed to uncover its location. Although the men have confessed to taking part in the robbery they have steadfastly refused to reveal the location of their hiding place. Authorities are—'" Greg stopped reading abruptly. "What do you think about that?" he asked.

"Do you suppose C. J. and Monte found out about this and think the silver is stashed around here somewhere?" Hip said.

The corners of Greg's mouth tightened. "Could be ... It just could be."

5

Greg Powell read the clipping a second time while his companions leaned forward, listening. "We don't know whether this is the reason C. J. and Monte have been hanging around here or not," he said when he finished, "but it's about the only decent clue we've got."

Hip's eyebrows contracted thoughtfully. "And it's not so hot, if you ask me."

"Nobody asked you," Greg countered, grinning.

His pal scowled. "Go fry an egg."

Greg was about to reply, but changed his mind. He guessed Hip was right. They could hardly call the clipping a real clue. After all, the incident had taken place more than 75 years before. Glumly he turned back to his reading.

Kim picked up a small handful of clippings she hadn't yet examined and directed her attention to them. "We're not finished yet," she said. "We'll find something else before we're through."

That was a possibility, Greg agreed, but the more clippings they went through without finding anything, the less encouraged he was. They found little that was even interesting to read, except a few articles about the Orientals. Hank read aloud an account of a tong war that had broken out between two rival Oriental factions.

"What's a tong?" Kim asked.

"I don't have a clue," Hank told her. "All I know is that there had been five men killed at the time this piece was written."

Kim shuddered.

Greg thought he remembered reading something about tongs and tong wars. He didn't know where, but it seemed to him that a tong was a secret club of Oriental men, and at times they had disagreements that led to fights.

"Sort of like what we call gangs now," he explained. "I don't think all tongs were bad, but some of them were into things like drugs, gambling and stealing."

"Maybe *that's* the connection," Hip put in, determined to build a mystery around the elderly Oriental man. "Maybe old Wai Chun Hing is a member of a tong and has a bunch of drugs hidden up here. Maybe C. J. and Monte found out about it and are trying to find them."

"I thought you said the old man was a kidnapper," Greg reminded him.

"Well . . . he probably peddles dope on the side."

They all laughed, except Kim. "I don't think it's a bit funny," she said. "He has to be a nice old man or he wouldn't have Somi living with him."

"Now you're sticking up for him. A little while ago you were storming because he wouldn't let her come to Sunday school."

"I still don't like that, but it's no reason to believe that he kidnapped her."

Hip grinned and in that instant Greg wondered if his pal had been kidding about the elderly man all along.

Quickly the smile faded and Greg couldn't be sure.

"We'd better get with it," Hank said, "or we won't be finished before dinner."

Hip picked up the clippings he still had to read. "Hey . . . look at this picture!"

"Wai Chun Hing!" they all chorused.

"Exactly! This is a story about one of the tongs. This guy was the leader at the time the picture was taken."

"It couldn't be the Wai Chun Hing we know," Greg protested, the initial excitement dying in his voice. "This picture was taken years and years and years ago. If it's the old Oriental's picture, he'd have to be about 150 years old by now."

"It's not of him, stupid!" Hip exclaimed. "It's his father!"

Greg took the clipping and examined it carefully. The man in the photo bore a startling resemblance to the elderly man who had taken Somi in. "It has to be his father!"

"I guess you're right," Hip said.

"I just thought of something!" Hank broke in. "Wai Chun Hing could tell us a lot about the days when there were many Orientals out here, and about tongs and their wars, too."

"If he *would*," Kim countered. "He wouldn't even let Somi speak to us a little while ago. I doubt that he would tell us anything."

Greg raised his gaze to look beyond the motor home, at the mountain that towered above it. "Why would we want to know anything about the days when there were a lot of Orientals out here?" he asked. "What would that have to do with C. J. and Monte?"

"One of the tongs might have hidden something around here," Hip put in. "If they had, and C. J. and Monte found out about it, they'd come on the double."

Greg laughed. "Listen to our detective!"

"Well, it could happen," the young Chicano replied.

"Maybe so, but who's going out to talk to Wai Chun Hing?"

"I thought you would," Hip said.

"Guess again. You're the one who's got the hot clue."

There was a brief silence. "I guess that isn't such a good idea after all."

Finally they finished reading the last of the clippings, put them back in the folder in their proper order and returned it to Mrs. Powell. It was almost supper time when Hank started home.

"You'll be here for Sunday school tomorrow, won't you?" Greg called after him.

"Like I told you," he said over his shoulder, "I'll try it once. That's all I'm promising."

That night the Powells and Hip Rodriguez spent a long while at family devotions praying about the Sunday school they were starting the next day. They were all concerned that they would have enough kids to make it interesting. It would be easier, they decided, if there were those who had gone to Sunday school regularly at some time during their lives and knew what they were missing, but there was only one—a girl Kim had invited. One or two others had been exposed to Sunday school and church briefly at one time or another, but that was all.

Nevertheless, the next day when time for Sunday school approached, the kids from the area flocked in. Kim and Greg looked over the crowd ecstatically. Eight or nine guys and girls who lived in the area were there, in addition to the Powells and Hip.

"Everybody's here!" Kevin exclaimed in a tense whisper.

Kim looked about the motor home again. "Not everybody." Disappointment crept into her voice.

"Who's missing?" Kevin asked.

"Somi."

"You didn't expect her, did you?"

Greg, who was sitting to his sister's left, hadn't expected the young Oriental either. He could still see the steel in Wai Chun Hing's eyes when the elderly man had come to the door and called Somi in. Anger and hate had mingled in his dark eyes and in the set of his handsome features. The man looked stern and uncompromising, as inflexible as an iron bar.

Mr. Powell called the kids to attention, welcomed them and asked Kim to lead in a song. Although "Jesus Loves Me" was a simple little tune that the Powell kids learned in their first year or two at Sunday school, few in the present group knew it. Next, Mrs. Powell taught them another favorite, "This Little Light of Mine." Greg led in prayer and Hip read Scripture. Then

Mr. Powell told a Bible story and applied the lessons to their daily lives. They listened intently and seemed surprised when the hour was over. Kevin closed the meeting in prayer.

Greg, who had been waiting tensely to find out how Hank liked it could finally wait no longer. He turned to his new friend. "Are you coming back next Sunday?"

The other boy's eyelids narrowed. "It wasn't too bad," he said. Then reluctantly, as though he was afraid to commit himself, he added, "But I'll have to wait and see how I feel when the time comes."

Greg's heart ached as his friend left with Arden and Scott. Although Hank had hedged about giving a definite answer, Greg thought he had read disapproval in his voice. He was sure Hank wouldn't be back for Sunday school next week. Somehow they had failed to reach him, in spite of all the prayers and the effort his folks had put into preparing that first meeting.

Greg remained in front of the motor home until the other guys turned up the path and disappeared from view. Only then was he aware that Hip and Kevin were beside him. "How'd Hank like it?" Hip asked.

Greg scowled and had to fight against a rising temper. For some reason he wanted to lash out angrily at his companions—to take his disappointment and frustration out on them. But even as emotion surged within him, he realized that it wasn't their fault that Hank had been so unresponsive. They would just have to love him a little more and pray harder for him.

"Hank claims he hasn't made up his mind yet," Greg said aloud, "so I don't know how he liked it."

"He'll be here," Hip replied firmly. "Now that he's been to Sunday school once, he won't be able to stay away."

While they were talking beside the motor home, a familiar brown oval face peered at them from a clump of brush on the edge of the clearing. The face was so small and unobtrusive Greg almost missed seeing it. However he happened to look in the right direction just as the silken black head appeared.

Although they were some distance away, Greg could easily read the hurt in those solemn features. His heart went out to the petite girl.

"Look," he murmured quietly to his companions as he tried not to let her know that he had seen her. "There's Somi. She must have slipped away from Wai Chun Hing and sneaked over to see what Sunday school is like."

"Where?" Kevin demanded, turning suddenly. As he did so she disappeared, moving quickly behind the dense screen of leaves.

"What do you suppose that was all about?" Hip asked.

Greg shook his head. There really was no way of knowing why Somi had been watching them. Yet, there was something about the incident that depressed him. He would have to talk to Kim again, he decided, and see if she would go over and give the girl another invitation to Sunday school.

His sister wasn't too anxious to do it, but when Greg volunteered to go along she said she would.

Greg thought about making the visit the following morning, but as the family was finishing breakfast there was a knock on the motor home door. Hank was there, his face flushed with excitement.

"Hey, Greg!" he called. "When are you comin' out?"

"Right away." Greg excused himself and joined his friend. Hip was half a step behind them.

"What's up?" Greg asked.

Hank motioned them away from the motor home with a quick jerk of his head.

"What's the deal?" Greg repeated when they were far enough from the vehicle to keep from being overheard.

"I saw C. J. and Monte at the store a little while ago," Hank said, keeping his voice tightly under control. "They had Mr. Heskett in a corner really talking to him."

"They weren't doing anything to him, were they?" Greg demanded. "If they were, we'll get Dad to call the sheriff."

"They weren't hurting him that I saw," Hank continued. "They were just standing there talking to him as though what they were saying was real important."

"Maybe they were threatening him," Hip said. "I wouldn't put anything past those guys."

Hank straightened. "What should we do about it?"

"We could go over and see what's goin' on," Greg suggested.

"You'll get us all in trouble," Hip protested.

"You can stay home if you want to," Hank told him.

"No way!"

"Come on, then," Greg exclaimed. "We've got to get over there quick!"

6

Greg and his companions left the little clearing on the run, angling up the steep mountain path in the direction of Poor Boy's Folly. The narrow trail was seldom used except by deer and elk, and an occasional mountain lion on the prowl for his dinner. Branches reached inward from either side of the path to claw at the boys. Greg felt the sleeve of his jacket tear and then felt the seering burn of a sharp branch on his arm.

Hank and Hip were a dozen paces or so behind and the distance was constantly growing as they walked more and more slowly. Greg had to wait for them when he reached the wider road.

"Do you suppose those guys are still at the store?" Hip asked.

Hank went out to the center of the road and peered down the long row of deserted buildings toward the general store standing alone at the far end. He nodded. "See, the car is still there!"

At first Greg couldn't see anything that even resembled a vehicle, but after a time he made out the thin edge of the car's rear bumper and trunk near the far corner of the store.

The boys moved up the road a dozen paces or so, then Greg grasped Hip's arm. "We're stupid to be going up the road this way. If those guys come out of the store, they'll spot us first thing."

At the thought of being caught again by those two, Hip almost leaped off the road in a frantic effort to hide. "You don't think they've already seen us, do you?"

Greg glowered at him. What a dumb question! How could they possibly know that? C. J. and Monte could be standing at the window right that instant watching them. They had no way of knowing until they reached the store themselves.

"How about it?" the young Chicano demanded.

"Maybe they've seen us," he replied, "and maybe not."

Hip swallowed against the lump that was growing in his throat. "Think we'd better go back and get your dad?" he stammered.

"We don't have time," Hank informed him tensely. "By the time we get back they'll be gone for sure."

"What's so bad about that?"

Greg and Hank acted as though they hadn't heard Hipolita. Greg motioned for his companions to follow as he started forward hurriedly, picking his way through the brush that lined the road.

"We'd better not go any closer," Hip murmured at last. For the last couple of hundred yards or so he had been lagging behind. "If those dudes hear us, they'll be out to nab us!"

Greg held up his hand in a signal for silence and his companions stopped suddenly.

"See anything?" Hank asked at last.

"Not yet," Greg whispered, "but the store's right across the road. We've got to be careful." A moment later he looked over his shoulder quickly. "Somebody's coming out of the building!"

Crouching even lower he inched forward, one stealthy step after another, moving up the steep slope to the very edge of the road. With only a thin wall of leaves protecting him and his companions from the view of the men who were standing just outside the building, he paused breathlessly, listening.

"Are you sure that's the part of town the coolies lived in?" Monte demanded roughly.

"I ought to be," they heard Mr. Heskett bristle. "Some of 'em were still around when I was a kid."

"If you're lyin', we'll be back!" Monte grabbed the elderly storekeeper by the shirt and hauled him close.

"Take your hands off me!"

Greg's lithe young body tensed and he moved forward without being aware of it, as though he was about to spring out of hiding and rush to the old man's defense.

"Take your hands off me!" Mr. Heskett repeated coldly.

"Come on, Monte," C. J. said. "Let him go."

The other man's grip relaxed and the elderly storekeeper wrenched free. "We'll let you go this time."

Greg peered out from behind the brush to see Mr. Heskett back off a step or two, still glaring at the man who had grabbed him. There was fear in his eyes, mingled with anger and frustration. "Don't you *ever* do that again."

"Monte's not going to hurt you, if you do as you're told," C. J. snarled. "And remember, if anybody asks you, you haven't seen us today."

Mr. Heskett nodded, the muscles in his face tightening.

The strangers started toward the car but Monte turned back for a moment. "If you say one word to anybody about this little talk of ours, we'll be back," he promised darkly.

C. J. was already in the car and had the motor started. He motioned impatiently for his companion to join him and a moment later they backed away from the store and went roaring up the road.

The boys remained in their hiding place for a minute or two.

"Now what?" Hip asked.

"Think we can find out anything by talking to the storekeeper?" Hank put in.

"Nope." Greg was still staring at the old man who had not moved since the strangers got into their car and drove away.

"He may know more than we think he does."

"Could be, but he's so scared he's not going to tell anybody anything."

Time seemed suspended, motionless.

"Those guys are up to something," Greg muttered. "And, whatever it is, it's not good."

"Let's go back where we can talk without being afraid Mr. Heskett will hear us," Hank said, turning and leading the others down the slope to the path they had left moments before.

When they could talk freely, Greg said, "I'd just as soon keep our being here right now a secret from everyone."

"Including Mr. Heskett?" Hank asked.

"Including Mr. Heskett. He wouldn't squeal on us but they might trick him into telling them. Those guys are slick." Greg paused momentarily, then found a fallen log where he sat down wearily. His companions flopped on the hard ground nearby.

"Now," he continued, "let's go over this whole affair from the beginning."

"That won't take long," Hip blurted. "What we know is a big, fat zero."

"We know those guys are tough," Hank said, shuddering. "And we know they're into something crooked."

"I think you're right," Greg said thoughtfully. He picked up a stone and threw it.

"First of all," Hip began, "we know that they came to the antique auction. They were right up front where everybody could see them."

"But they didn't buy anything," Hip put in.

"That's right. They didn't buy anything. In fact, it didn't seem to me as though they were even interested in buying anything. That's mystery number one."

"And mystery number two is that they didn't want their pictures taken," Hank said. "Why?"

"Maybe they're wanted by the police," Hip suggested.

"That's the first thing a guy would think of, but there might be some other reason."

"Like what?" Hip demanded skeptically.

"Search me." Greg shrugged and for a time fell silent. "Now we've got three more mysteries. Why did C. J. and Monte come back to the ghost town after they made it so plain that they were going back to Denver?"

"And why did they want to know where the Oriental workers had lived in Poor Boy's Folly?" Hank asked. "That's another mystery."

"And finally, why didn't they want anyone to know that they had been in the ghost town today?"

Hip's eyes shone. "It sounds to me as though we've got a real, sure-enough mystery on our hands."

"You can say that again," Greg replied, breaking a twig off the nearest bush and using the pencil-sized stick to mark the hard soil of the path. "The question is, where do we go from here? How do we go about unraveling this mess?"

His companions shook their heads.

"What do you think?" Hank wanted to know.

Greg didn't have any idea either as to why C. J. and Monte had been acting as they had. The information he and his pals had was so disjointed it didn't make sense. Still, there had to be a logical explanation for all that had happened. Somehow each fact was related to the others like the bricks in a wall. Only there was no apparent pattern yet.

"I keep wondering why C. J. and Monte wanted to know which part of town the Orientals had lived in," Greg said at last. "That seems to be important to them for some reason."

"And," Hip put in, "they were so anxious to keep Mr. Heskett from telling anyone about their visit today. I think those two facts are linked together."

Both Hank and Greg agreed with him.

"But we're not going to get any info from Mr. Heskett," Hank observed.

"How about your dad, Hank?" Greg asked. "He knows a lot about the old days. Maybe he could help us figure out why those two guys would be so interested in the Orientals who used to live here."

"It's been a long time since there were many of them around," Hank said.

"There is somebody who could help us," Hip said reluctantly, "if he only would!"

"Wai Chun Hing!" Greg exclaimed.

"He'll know, all right," Hip added, "but there's a catch. He might work us over before we have a chance to tell him what we want to know."

"It wouldn't hurt to try," Greg said. "We're going over to see him again about letting Somi come to our Sunday school anyway."

Hank's eyelids slitted narrowly. "That's a waste of time, too. He worships his ancestors. You won't catch him buying that Christianity bit."

"Worships his ancestors?" Hip echoed. "You've got to be kidding!"

"No way. He's got this little church, or whatever you call it, right in his house and he kneels down every day and prays to his dead relatives. My dad was telling me about it."

Greg and Hip shivered. "You don't suppose he's got Somi doing that, too, do you?" the Powell boy asked.

"You can bet on it."

"We can't have her worshiping her dead family. We've got to get her to Sunday school."

Greg agreed with his friend, but working things out wasn't going to be that easy.

"We could get Kim to try and see Somi or Wai Chun Hing about it," he said aloud.

Hank shrugged indifferently. "It won't do any good."

Kim was still at the motor home when the boys returned. She went with them to the neat little house where the Oriental man and Somi lived. The foursome was some distance away when they saw smoke spiraling upward among the trees, a mute indication that the old man, at least, was home.

"I guess we lucked out," Greg said.

"Maybe," Hank answered doubtfully.

"He's home, isn't he?"

When Greg had first caught a glimpse of the house he had been sure the front door was ajar and the shades were up. But by the time the group had reached the clearing, the door was closed and the shades were drawn tight against the curious stares of anyone approaching the trim little building. Greg knew, even before they knocked, that Wai Chun Hing would not come to the door.

7

That night at devotions the Powells prayed a long time for Somi. The news that Wai Chun Hing worshiped his ancestors and was probably teaching her to do the same gave an urgency to getting her to their Sunday school.

"The problem is really Wai Chun Hing," Greg said, his own irritation showing through. "We don't have a chance of getting her to come as long as he won't let us talk to her."

"That's for sure," Hip exclaimed, pulling in a deep breath. "I can hardly stand it when I think that he's teaching her to bow down to a fat, ugly Buddha and worship her own ancestors or those of the old man she lives with."

"I feel the same," Mr. Powell replied, "but we've got to remember that they worship the way they do because they don't know any different. That's why it's so important that we take the gospel to them. If we don't, they'll die in their sin."

The kids looked from one to another with growing uneasiness. The silence was electrifying.

"How come Somi is staying with old Wai Chun Hing?" Kevin wanted to know. "He isn't even a relative."

"I was talking with Hank's mother," Mrs. Powell began. "She told me what she knows of the story."

Somi was from Thailand and wasn't sure what had happened to her parents, but she believed they had been killed. Somi's mother's sister had taken her in, adopted her and brought her to Colorado with them.

"Oh," Kim said, "so that's it." She seemed more interested in the story than anyone else.

"Then," Mrs. Powell went on, "Somi's aunt took sick and had to have major surgery. She didn't respond to treatment, but kept getting weaker and weaker. Finally the doctor insisted that she move to a lower altitude and let someone else take care of the children.

"She had three of her own, so those three went to live with her husband's sister and Wai Chun Hing took Somi," Christine Powell concluded.

"Will she ever go back to them?"

Mrs. Powell shook her head. "I couldn't tell you."

"It makes us feel a little more kindly toward Wai Chun Hing, doesn't it?" Mr. Powell said. "He didn't have to take her in."

"If only he'd let us talk to her about going to Sunday school," Kevin said.

"We'll have to pray about that."

The following morning Hank was back at the motor home before the breakfast dishes were finished. As soon as the Powell kids and Hip had their morning chores done they joined him once more. This time Kim went along.

"What're we going to do now?" she asked curiously.

"Find out what this mystery is about," Hip said.

"And just how are we going to do that?"

"I've been doing a lot of thinking," Greg said. "You know, when we were talking about the mystery surrounding C. J. and Monte, we forgot about the night of the auction when we saw them drive back to the edge of town and hide their car in the brush."

Hank's eyes widened. "And they went on into town on foot."

"Exactly . . . I figure they did that so they could explore the buildings without anyone knowing about it."

A squirrel chattered at them from his perch on a branch overhead and the kids turned to look at him. Only after the happy, noisy little creature darted to the other side of the tree trunk and down to the ground did anyone speak.

"Are you thinking what I'm thinking?" Hip asked.

"That we look through those buildings to see if we can find any clues?" Greg guessed.

His pal grimaced. "I must be getting soft in the head even to think such a thing. They'll probably catch us and tie us up in one of the deepest mines on the mountain—so far down we'll *never* be able to get out!"

"Don't talk that way!" Kim exclaimed, shivering.

"Well, they might."

Greg grinned. "You can stay here if you want to. Hank and I'll go look."

"No way," Hip retorted quickly. "We may be scared, but we're not missing out on all the fun, are we, Kim?"

"I—I guess not."

Kevin came out of the motor home at that moment and joined them. "Wherever it is you're going," he announced firmly, "I'm going along."

"Says who?" Greg demanded.

"Says me." He found a place on the other end of the log and sat down. "I can tell you're planning something."

The other kids looked at each other and then back at Greg. For a moment he didn't know what to say. He didn't really care if his younger brother joined them, but that made five in their party. It would be just that much harder to hide and that much easier for the men to grab one of them, if it came to either possibility. Still, if they didn't let him tag along he might make such a fuss about being left behind that their folks might decide not to let any of them go.

"You won't get scared, will you?" Greg wanted to know.

Kevin pulled himself erect, indignation blazing in his eyes. "Me, scared?" he echoed.

"And you won't bug us to turn around and go home, will you?"

"How many times do I have to tell you? I'm not going to be any more scared than you are."

"Is that a promise?"

"Oh, man!" Kevin moaned to no one in particular. "This is stupid! . . . Of course it's a promise."

"OK." Greg turned to the others. "If it's all right with the rest of you, it's OK with me."

They all nodded solemnly.

They made their way up to the abandoned ghost town. They stopped uneasily near the battered sign that had once so proudly announced the village limits of Poor Boy's Folly.

"What're we going to do?" Kevin asked.

"I thought you knew," his older brother said. "We're going through some of the old buildings to see if we can find any clues as to why C. J. and Monte are still hanging around up here."

The younger boy gasped.

"No backing out!" Greg reminded him.

Kevin's cheeks paled, but his voice was bold. "Who's backing out? I'm just surprised, that's all!"

"You and me both," Hip told him. "I'm not only surprised that I'm up here, I'm scared. I keep asking myself how I could be so stupid."

His remark seemed to break the tension and they all laughed.

"Let's get movin'," Greg said, starting in the direction of the ghost town, "before those dudes show up again."

With some hesitation they opened the door of the first building and stepped inside.

"I can't see a thing," Kevin said.

They waited with growing uneasiness for their eyes to grow accustomed to the semi-darkness of the dank, dust-ridden interior. At one time there had been a hasp and heavy padlock on the front door, but those had long since given way to the ravages of time and the efforts of the curious and mischievous. The door sagged on its hinges.

The wide boards of the floor were warped by 70 years of swelling and shrinking with the coming of rains and long dry periods, and the refuse of men long forgotten still cluttered the room.

"There's sure nothing in here worth stealing," Greg said. He held his flashlight in his hand, ready for use if necessary. His dad had taught him to use it sparingly to save the batteries.

Kevin crossed the creaking floor and opened a closet. The door squeaked in protest and the bottom of it hung up on a warped floorboard. He had to lift it to get it open. "There's nothing in here worth stealing either," he added.

"Now that I think of it," Greg said, "we're not going to find anything out in the open. Stuff like that would have been taken a long time ago. And, as much prowling around as C. J. and Monte have done the last few days, they'd have located anything easy to find."

"You've got something there," Hip replied. Disappointment edged his voice. "But there's some reason for them to be doing what they're doing."

"I'm not ready to give up yet," Hank put in.

"Neither am I. We've just got to quit looking in the more obvious places. We'll have to try to find the kind of secretive spots a person might use for hiding something valuable."

"And just where would that be?"

"We won't know for sure until we find it."

Hip shook his head. "That's a lot of help. Really neat."

They went over the main floor using Greg's powerful flashlight to pry into the dark recesses of the closets and the cupboards in the kitchen. They found a box or two stashed away, and for an instant were excited about them, but they were empty.

At last they concluded that the first building had nothing of value in it. With diminishing hope they moved to the store beside it. There were big bay windows across the front, with space for displays behind them. The main room stretched almost to the rear, with a small storage area behind that, and a door that led to the basement. The main floor was completely empty.

"Nothing here, either," Kim observed.

Greg's flashlight beam sought out the basement stairs at one side of the storage room. "How about it? Do we go down?"

"My feet say no," Hip murmured, "but we've got to find out what's at the bottom of all this."

The flashlight stabbed a feeble yellow hole in the gloom of the windowless cellar beneath the old store building. Cobwebs were hanging from the floor joists and streaming down the corners of the walls. At the bottom of the stairs the kids paused nervously.

"Places like this give me the creeps," Hank whispered.

"Me, too," Kevin said, his voice quavering. "If those guys come back here, we're done for! There's no way out of here except up those stairs!"

"You could've talked all day without saying that," Hip replied with a nervous laugh.

At that instant there was a sudden crackling sound above them—a door slamming, or loose shutters banging in the wind. Kim gasped and reached out impulsively to clamp her fingers on her younger brother's wrist. As she touched him, he yelped aloud.

"Quiet!" Greg ordered. In spite of his efforts to be firm and authoritative, there was a faint tremolo in his words. "If C. J. and Monte are anywhere around they're sure to find us with all your shouting."

By this time Kevin realized it was his sister's hand on his arm and he turned indignantly to her. "After this, keep your hands to yourself!"

She giggled.

"There's nothing funny about it! You could give a guy a heart attack."

"Come on, you two," Greg ordered. He was once more in command of the situation. "Let's look over this cellar and get out of here before somebody does come. OK?"

They moved silently about the dark, musty cellar, peering into boxes piled in one corner and shelves along one wall.

"There's sure nothing down here that's worth stealing," Hip said at last. "Let's go."

"That's the best idea I've heard all morning," Kevin replied. Even as he spoke he turned and would have started up the stairs but his brother stopped him.

"Just a minute," Greg exclaimed, bringing the shaft of light back to the wall beyond the shelves. "What's that?"

"I don't see anything."

"That stuff on the wall. It looks like some kind of a little red shelf."

For a moment they stared at it. It was small and very old, with the dust of decades still clinging to it. It had been put up for some special purpose; that was apparent. But it was empty now, save for a small, handleless cup of sand or dirt sitting in front, on the very edge.

"What do you suppose it was for?" Kim asked curiously.

"Maybe they used it for candles when they came down here to get something," Hip suggested.

However she didn't think so. "I don't believe they used candles much around here in those days, did they, Hank?"

"I don't think so. Dad always talked about kerosene lamps and lanterns. I suppose some people used candles, but I'm sure there weren't very many."

Greg had to agree with his sister and Hank. There were quite a few bent nails sticking down from the joists in several places around the basement that looked as though they had been used to hang lanterns from. That shelf had been put up for some purpose very important to the store owner, Greg was sure. Nobody would put up anything just for decoration in a cellar like this one.

He took the cup from the shelf and examined it under his flashlight. It was filled with sand and there were several tiny, slender pieces of wood sticking from it—wood that had been coated with some soft brown substance until it was the size of a Fourth of July sparkler, or a little bigger.

"I can't figure it out," he said, returning the cup to the shelf.

"Neither can the rest of us," Kevin blurted. "Now, let's get out of here."

They all started for the stairs.

8

The next building was obviously a saloon. The swinging doors had been taken down and replaced with heavy, homemade closures, but there was no mistaking the original purpose of the structure. There was a bar along one side with shelves for bottles behind it.

A huge mirror had once graced the center of the wall, framed by shelving, but it had long since been broken. Only a jagged triangle of silvered glass remained in place. Some of the tables and chairs had been taken out but a few broken ones remained, scattered carelessly about the rest of the narrow room.

"I'm beginning to think we were mistaken about C. J. and Monte. Maybe there isn't anything around here worth taking," Greg said.

They were in the center of the room trying to decide whether to go home or on to the hotel building next door when they heard something outside. It was a dull, muted sound that drifted faintly into the empty saloon.

Kevin jerked himself about. "What was that?"

"S-S-Sh!" Greg whispered tautly.

"Is there somebody out there?" Kim asked, her throat dry and hoarse.

Greg and Hank did not reply. They were leaning forward slightly, listening.

Hip crushed close to the front door, his head cocked to one side. "Yep," he whispered. "There's somebody out there!"

"Oh, man!" Kevin breathed.

"But I don't think they're coming in here."

"I just thought of something," Hank said. "There's no back door out of this building any more. It's boarded up."

"Maybe there's no back door now," Kevin announced, "but if somebody comes in the front I'm goin' to make a back door—but fast!"

Quietly the older boys edged toward the door and peeked out. "We *are* getting jumpy," Greg said. "It's only Somi."

Kim moved up beside him and peered over his shoulder. "Look at that armload of groceries she's carrying."

"And she's got a long way to go," Hip said, concern creeping into his voice.

"We can't let her carry them all alone," Kim said, opening the door and stepping out into the bright sunlight. "I'm going to help her."

At the sound of their voices Somi turned, a smile lighting her brown oval face.

"You've got a big load there," Kim told her.

She shifted the sack from one arm to the other. "I've carried more than this lots of times," she explained.

"Let us help you."

"I can manage," she protested.

"But it will be easier if you have help." Kim's smile was warm as she took the large sack from Somi.

"Grandfather doesn't like to have me carry so much, but he can't do it with his rheumatism and everything."

"When you have to go for groceries," the older girl replied, "let me know and I'll go along to help carry them."

"So'll I," Kevin put in. He glanced at his companions as he spoke, warning them with his eyes to keep any bright remarks to themselves.

They hadn't gone far when Greg took the groceries from his sister. It was Hank's turn next, then Hip's and finally Kevin's. Before long they were at the home of the elderly Oriental.

"Thank you so much," she said, taking the sack again in her arms. "I didn't carry it at all. That doesn't seem right."

"Maybe it will help to make up for all the times you had to carry them alone," Hip told her.

Before she could reply, the front door opened and Wai Chun Hing stepped out. His movements, restricted by arthritis, were painfully slow. "Is everything all right?" he asked.

"Yes, Grandfather," Somi answered quickly. "These friends helped me carry the groceries home, that's all."

He seemed surprised at that. For an instant incredulity flecked his dark eyes. Then the hard lines of his sunken features softened and a faint smile glowed on his face. He drew his frail torso erect and bowed slightly from the waist.

"I wish to thank you for being so gracious to my little Somi," he said. "It is far to the store and the sacks get heavy before she is home. It was so kind of you to help her do something I can no longer do."

He was so formal they eyed him uncomfortably. Greg and the others thought he was dismissing them and started to leave, but he stopped them. "As I said, I would go after our food myself if I could, but these tired arms and legs of mine can no longer make it up the hill to Mr. Heskett's store. So, reluctantly, I have to depend upon the little one."

"I don't mind, Grandfather," Somi broke in quickly.

"I know you don't, my dear." His smile escaped the prison of his will and burst across his face. "But the task is still most difficult for you and I am very grateful for the help these—these friends of yours have given you ... Do you think they would like to come in and have some tea and cookies?" Although he was speaking to Somi his attention was directed at Kim and the boys.

"That sounds great," Kevin exclaimed.

Wai Chun Hing held the door open while they filed in. For a moment they stood just inside. They had never been in a house that looked quite like this one. It was exquisitely furnished, with a thick wool rug of intricate design reaching from one wall to the other. The chairs and sofa were massive, hand-carved works of art and a tall oriental screen of teak, ivory, jade and silk separated the dining area from the living room.

"Wow!" Kevin muttered under his breath. He was about to step farther into the room but Somi stopped him with a quick warning glance.

"It is our custom to take off our shoes when we come into the house," she said quietly.

Cheeks flushing, Kevin stooped quickly and untied his tennis shoes so he could slip out of them. The others did the same, while Wai Chun Hing smiled his approval. It was obvious that he looked upon the act as a sign of good breeding.

"Our humble home is honored by your presence," he said. Seating them in the living room he excused himself and hobbled into the kitchen.

Almost immediately Somi got to her feet. "Please excuse me," she said, "but I must help Grandfather."

Greg glanced about the room. There was a beautiful painting of long-legged birds on the wall, so realistically formed they looked as though one powerful stroke of their wings would be enough to lift them from the canvas and soar out among the trees, clouds and the smiling sun. An embroidered picture hung on the opposite wall and beneath it, on a small table near the lamp, stood a small, delicate-featured figurine of an aged woman, back bent with work.

Then Greg saw it. A small red shelf like the one he and his companions had seen earlier in the store cellar. Only the one in Wai Chun Hing's home was more ornate and brightly painted. A small Buddha looked down at Greg from its perch at the back of the shelf. And before it, stood the small cup of sand with the brown coated sticks protruding from it. The sticks were glowing as they sent up an overpowering sweet-scented smoke.

Greg had never seen a Buddhist shrine before, but he recognized it immediately—even before he saw the offerings of fruit, oil and food on the floor in front of it. A terrible revulsion swept over him.

He turned deliberately so he couldn't see it. Yet it was etched deeply on the screen of his mind.

Oddly enough, he thought more about the god shelf in the basement of the abandoned store. He could see the Orientals who owned the place, or worked there, stumbling down the steep steps, joss sticks and food offerings in their hands. He could see the flickering light as the matches caught and could smell the sickening sweet stench of incense as the brown sticks ignited. Now that he had smelled it once he knew he would never forget it. And he could see them prostrate themselves on the cold floor as they placed their food offerings for the relatives who had died before them.

Greg saw that Hip and the others were also staring at the god shelf with its Buddha, its smoking joss sticks and its food offerings. He hoped they wouldn't say anything to offend their sensitive, gentle host, yet he had to admit that he would understand if they did. He didn't think he had ever been so bewildered and disturbed about anything as he was at seeing the pagan place of worship.

A few moments later Somi and her grandfather returned with a pot of lightly brewed green tea that tasted but little different than hot water, and a plate of delicate, wafer-thin cookies that were delicious.

Wai Chun Hing was warm and gracious in spite of the fact that he said little, except in direct response to their questions. Near the end of their unexpected visit he spoke again of their kindness in helping Somi carry home the big sack of groceries.

Then Kim, who had been waiting for an opportunity, asked if Somi could come to Sunday school. She did so gravely, as though the invitation had never been given before. Disapproval flashed in the old man's eyes, but only for an instant. Then they softened slightly and Greg thought he saw a thin smile toying with the corners of Wai Chun Hing's mouth.

"We will speak of the matter, Somi and I," he said. There was a finality in his voice that told his guests that there was to be no more discussion then.

The old man followed them to the door and waited quietly for them to put on their shoes.

"Stop anytime," he said as they left. "Somi's friends are always welcome."

In spite of the warmth that had been present in the old man's manner the kids were still not sure he would let Somi come to Sunday school.

"You saw the way he looked when we asked," Hip said. "He doesn't want her to, that's for sure."

"Maybe not," Kim replied, "but I still think he'll let her." There was a brief pause. "We've been praying about it every night. God's going to answer our prayers."

The next morning the Powells and Hip were bustling around the motor home getting ready for Sunday school when there was a timid knock at the door. Kim opened it to see Somi standing there.

"Hello." Her voice was as faint as her smile.

"I'm so glad to see you," Kim exclaimed. "Come in."

For an instant Somi remained motionless, as though uncertain whether to accept the invitation. She was dressed in a pair of clean jeans and a blue denim shirt with a light jacket over it to block out the morning chill.

"I—" Her voice trailed off uneasily.

"Come in," Kim repeated.

Somi stepped inside timorously and stooped to loosen her sandals.

"You don't have to take off your shoes in here," Kim told her. "See. We're all wearing our shoes."

She looked up. "Grandfather would not like it if I come into your home without taking off my shoes," she protested. "He says it is not good manners to track dirt into a house."

Kim might have argued with that but her mother came over just then. "If you feel better taking off your shoes, my dear, then by all means, take them off."

Somi smiled gratefully.

No one found out whether or not she enjoyed Sunday school. She sat stiffly on a chair next to Kim without taking part. And when the service was over she thanked Mrs. Powell and Kim and was gone, darting like a frightened fawn down the narrow trail toward her home.

"Well," Greg said, "she came after all. I wondered if she would."

"So did I," his dad answered. "Suppose she'll be back next Sunday?"

Bernard Palmer

Hurt leaped to Kim's eyes and for a moment she looked as though she was about to cry. "Don't you suppose she will?"

Her dad put an arm about her shoulder. "We'll have to pray that she will, won't we?" he asked.

"I'm going over to see her next week," she retorted firmly. "I'm going every chance I get."

The Powells had been so concerned about Somi they didn't notice that Hank Wendland had stayed behind after Sunday school until he spoke.

"Why do you care whether she comes to Sunday school or not?" he asked curiously.

Greg turned to face him. At first he thought his friend was taunting Kim. Then he realized that he was serious.

"What do you mean?" he asked.

Hank sauntered to the far end of the motor home and leaned against it. For a time he stared down the trail where Somi had just disappeared. "You go to all that work having Sunday school," he said. "If she's stupid enough not to want to come, why worry? Let her bug out if she wants to."

Greg hesitated, embarrassment staining his cheeks.

"How come?" Hank repeated.

"We want her to have a chance to receive Christ, too," he said at last.

His new friend shook his head. "I don't get it."

"That's the reason we have Sunday school in the first place," Greg explained.

"You're weird!"

9

Greg and Hip expected Hank to come over to the motor home on Monday morning about the time they finished breakfast as he usually did, but this time he didn't show. They didn't see him until almost noon.

"Where've you been?" Hip exclaimed when he saw him. "We were worried about you."

"I'll bet." He leaned against the side of the motor home, a grin playing with the corners of his mouth.

"Kim was," Hip added teasingly.

Hank's cheeks flushed and he scowled at the young Chicano but said nothing.

"Well . . . where've you been?" Greg broke in.

"What makes you think I've been anywhere?"

"You had to be or you'd have come over." He lowered his voice. "We were going to do some more detective work. Remember?"

Hank nodded as he moved some distance from the rear of the vehicle. "It so happens that I *was* doing some detective work," he whispered.

The boys crowded close around him.

"I went to the county seat with Dad to get license plates for our new truck. While we were in the courthouse we heard some news about Poor Boy's Folly."

"Yes?" Greg said, his tone urging Hank on.

"C. J. and Monte have bought the old hotel, the store with the altar in the cellar and the two buildings in between."

"You're puttin' us on!" Greg's voice rose with disbelief.

"No way. And that's not all. They've taken an option to buy some land right behind the ghost town . . . ." Seeing the disbelief in his friends' eyes he continued, "They were in the courthouse this morning getting the papers recorded. I saw them myself."

Hip whistled in amazement. "Man, that's weird!"

"But what would they do with those old buildings and a chunk of mountain land you can't raise anything on?" Greg asked skeptically.

"That's what Dad asked the guy in the courthouse," Hank continued. "He said he didn't know, but he thought they were going to fix up the buildings to take tourists and have some horses for them to ride."

The boys turned that over in their minds.

"Big deal!" Hip exclaimed in disgust. "That means those guys'll be around all summer."

"I can't buy all that," Greg muttered. "Those two aren't going to start any kind of business they'd have to work at."

Hip picked up a twig and broke it with his fingers. "I've got to agree with you."

"Me, too," Hank replied.

"Only why are they going to all that trouble?" Greg wanted to know.

"Like we said," Hip continued, "they may figure there's some stolen silver in one of those old buildings."

"Or," Hank added, "maybe they've found a new mine."

"They could be figuring some kind of scheme to make people think they've found more silver so they can talk them into investing in it."

"That sounds more like it," Hipolita said, sighing deeply. "Only how are we going to find out for sure?"

"Well," Hank replied, "we're not going to find out anything staying here. That's for sure."

"Only we can't go up there this afternoon," Greg said. "Dad left some work for us to do."

Disappointment clouded Hank's eyes. "Tomorrow?"

"Tomorrow morning."

"Early."

Greg and Hip carried water from the nearby stream, washed the motor home and waxed it. Kevin came up when they were almost done and helped them. As they were finishing, Mrs. Powell called them to supper.

"Well," George Powell said when they were all at the table. "I've got a little news about your friends."

Greg looked up. "You mean C. J. and Monte?"

"I'd hate to see a dude ranch up here," Mr. Powell went on, "but I suppose they have as much right to come in here as anyone else."

Greg leaned forward slightly. He was about to ask his dad a question when there was a sudden hammering at the door and it flew open. Somi came bursting in, her eyes wide with fear. "Kim! Mrs. Powell! Come quick! Grandfather—"

Christine Powell leaped to her feet. "What's wrong?" she demanded.

"It's Grandfather!" Tears welled up in the slight, dark-skinned girl's almond eyes. "He couldn't get up for supper tonight and that's never happened before." Her lips quivered. "And he hurts so bad!"

Mrs. Powell swept her into her arms and held her close for an instant. "There now," she said, "we'll go over and see what we can do to help him."

Somi's gaze met Mrs. Powell's.

"Want to take the pickup?" George asked. "Or do you want me along?"

"I might need your help," she said softly.

"I'm going, too," Kim announced.

Mr. Powell got his jacket and started for the door. He stopped, however, and asked the boys to pray for them and Wai Chun Hing.

They were bowing their heads as their parents and the two girls got into the pickup and drove away.

It was long after dark when Mr. Powell and Kim returned. They had gone to the old Oriental's home and found the situation just as Somi had said it was. Mrs. Powell tried to make him comfortable while George drove to the Heskett store to phone for an ambulance to take the elderly man to the hospital. When it arrived Somi insisted on going along so Mrs. Powell went, too.

"I'll go in tomorrow morning and see how things are," Mr. Powell said.

"Do you think it's serious?" Greg wanted to know.

He shook his head. "All I know is that he can't get up and is in terrible pain."

"Can I go back to the hospital with you tomorrow?" Kim asked seriously.

He reached over and rumpled her hair. "I reckon so."

Hank Wendland arrived at the motor home the next morning as Mr. Powell and Kim were pulling away. Greg told him about the elderly Oriental man taking sick and about his mother going to the hospital to stay with Somi.

For an instant Hank's frown deepened. "Somi and Wai Chun Hing are no relation to you. Why get all hyped up about them?"

"They need us," Greg said simply.

"Come on, you guys," Hip broke in, starting up the trail.

"What's the rush?" Hank grumbled.

"You were the one who wanted to start early," Hip reminded him.

After locking the motor home securely, they started up the narrow, twisting trail in the direction of the ghost town.

"Think C. J. and Monte'll be there this morning?" Kevin asked uncertainly.

"No way," Hip retorted.

"That's what you say, but if they are around, it'll be a real bummer."

"Think positive, Kev. Think positive."

"It's not the thinking that worries me," the younger boy said. "It's what we'll find when we get up there . . . Maybe a whole mess of trouble."

"And we might find the answers to all the questions that have been bugging us," Hank observed.

"Or maybe we'll find a couple of mean dudes who'd just as soon chop us into little pieces as look at us."

"We're not going to get into any trouble," Greg said. "That I'll guarantee." He pulled in a long breath. "And we'd better stop this kind of talk or we'll split before we have a chance to find out anything."

"That," Hip murmured, "would be crude."

Greg fingered the camera suspended by a strap around his neck, drawing Kevin's attention to it for the first time that morning.

"You brought *that* along?" the younger boy said in disgust.

"My new Polaroid." He held the camera up to his eyes, as though about to snap the shutter. "Should I take your picture?"

"It was your other new camera that almost got us into trouble with C. J. and Monte the first time we saw them!" Kevin reminded him fiercely.

"I know . . . But today if they yell about me taking their pictures I'll just hand the print to them. That way I won't lose a whole roll."

The others laughed, but Kevin didn't. "You can joke about it if you want to," he said, "but

I don't want to be ripped off by those dudes again."

They had been walking as they talked and were now making their way up the hard-packed street toward the long-vacant buildings.

"Hey," Greg said as they neared the store where they had found the ornate altar in the cellar. "We've got time to go in here for a minute, haven't we?"

"What for?" Hank wanted to know.

"I'd like to go down in the cellar and get a couple of shots of that god shelf or Oriental altar or whatever you call it."

"You can't take a picture down there," Kevin said.

"I've got my trusty flash along," Greg reminded him.

"I'd just as soon do what we've got to do and get out of here," Kevin growled. Nevertheless, he was the first in the store. He made his way to the back of the narrow structure and would have led the way down to the cellar except that Greg had the flashlight.

The yellow beam of light bored a hole in the blackness below, revealing the cobwebbed beams and a thin strip of hard-packed dirt floor.

Hip shuddered. "I'm with you, Kev," he said. "The sooner we can get out of here the better. This place gives me the creeps."

"Me, too," the younger Powell boy said, grateful for company in his growing uneasiness.

"It'll only take a couple of minutes," Greg said handing the flashlight to Hank who was next to him. "Shine it on that shelf so I can focus. OK?"

He took two or three pictures and was stuffing them in his shirt pocket when the front door of the crusty building squealed protestingly.

"Someone's coming!" Greg whispered. "Douse the light!"

As heavy footsteps sounded on the rough flooring above, Hank found the flashlight switch with trembling fingers and snapped off the brilliant beam of light.

"I don't like the idea of comin' in here like this, C. J.," a voice the boys recognized as Monte's complained. "Somebody's apt to spot us in broad daylight like this."

"Who's got a better right to be here? Answer me that! We just bought the place—all legal and proper. It belongs to us."

"That's another thing I can't dig," Monte protested irritably. "Spending all that bread on a bunch of junk that's apt to fall down before we're done with it."

"Don't get so uptight. Buying those buildings was the smartest thing we ever did."

"Says you."

"Wait 'til the deal's over. You'll be saying so yourself."

"Maybe," Monte continued, "but I still don't like the idea of bein' up here ... Look how those blasted kids are snoopin' around all the time."

"That's just your imagination," C. J. said angrily. "They're just ordinary kids foolin' around like kids do."

"Don't try to tell me that. You've seen the way they look at us. They're onto something and don't you forget it!"

C. J.'s words were hard and iced. "If they get in our way, they'll be sorry."

"You can say that again!" Monte cursed savagely. "I'll take care of 'em myself."

In the basement the kids crouched fearfully, their breath coming in thin, shallow gasps. Greg was sure the men upstairs would hear them and groped for Hip's arm to warn him with a squeeze of his fingers. His pal jumped at the touch and almost cried out in terror.

"Forget those kids," C. J. said. "We've got work to do."

"Move the car around to the back," Monte replied. "I'll pry the boards off the back door so we can get it open."

"OK, but be careful. After we get that stuff down the cellar we've got to be able to lock this place up so tight not even a mouse can get in."

"And those pesky kids!"

They heard C. J. retreating to the front door while Monte went to work prying off the heavy planking that barred the rear door.

"They're coming down here!" Kevin exclaimed hoarsely. "And we can't get away from them. We're trapped!"

Greg shivered and was suddenly icy cold. What his younger brother said was true. There was only one way out of the cellar and Monte was standing within ten feet of the top of the stairs.

10

"Those guys'll be down here any minute!" Hip whispered. "What're we goin' to do?"

"We could make a break for it while C. J.'s outside," Greg suggested. "That way some of us'd get away to go and tell Dad. He'd get the sheriff and arrest those dudes."

"Dad's at the hospital," Kevin said tautly.

"Then, the guys who get away could go to Hank's. His dad'd fix their plow soon enough."

"But my folks are gone this morning, too."

Kevin groaned inwardly.

"I don't know what we ought to do," Hip said, keeping his voice soft, "but whatever it is, we'd better do it quick!"

At that instant there was a loud knock on the rear door, followed by C. J.'s muffled tones. Greg couldn't hear exactly what he was saying, but he was sure they were talking about getting the back door open in a hurry so they could get down the cellar.

"Just hang loose, C. J.!" Monte called out a moment later, verifying Greg's suspicion. "I've only got a few more spikes to pull and we'll be in business."

A quick, silent prayer escaped Greg's lips as a big nail squealed in protest at being jerked from its mooring.

"Give me the flashlight," Hank said quickly. "And follow me!"

"Where?"

"We'll talk later!"

Mutely the boys tiptoed across the floor to the far corner of the cellar. Hank indicated with a motion of the light that they should re-pile the boxes that had been stacked there. Greg didn't know what it was all about, but like his new friend said, there was no time to talk about it right then.

The boys set to work hurriedly, lifting one empty wooden crate after another, piling them to one side. Upstairs, they heard the long-closed back door open.

"It's about time," C. J. grumbled.

At the sound of his voice Kevin dropped a box with a dull thud. Silence gripped the men on the main floor.

"What was that?" Monte demanded uneasily.

For an instant there was no sound from either of the men.

"Think we ought to go down and check it out?" Monte asked at last.

"The place is alive with rats," C. J. said.

"I could go down and see."

"Let's get the stuff unloaded first."

By this time the yellow beam of light in Hank's hand revealed a small trapdoor level with the floor.

"OK," Hank whispered. "While I get this open, pull a couple of boxes close so I can reach 'em with the door open."

Greg didn't know what his friend was planning but did as he was told. Hurriedly the boys scrambled into the dark opening. Just as the men were coming down the rickety stairs, Hank pulled the boxes over so they were resting on the trapdoor. He was as careful as possible closing the door, yet it still made a dull thudding sound that seemed to echo through the cellar.

"What was that?" Monte cried again, loudly enough for the boys to hear.

"Don't be so jumpy!" C. J. retorted. "It was just those rats."

"It didn't sound like *four-legged* rats to me," Monte muttered darkly.

"Look for yourself," C. J. said. "But at least get off the stairs so I can set this box down. It's heavy!"

Monte still was not satisfied—or so it seemed to the frightened kids. "Those boxes aren't the way we left 'em!" he grumbled, his tone suspicious. "Somebody could've gone through that trapdoor into the tunnel."

"You *are* getting jumpy," C. J. said, laughing. "Come on, we've got work to do. We don't want anybody catching us today."

"And we don't want nobody coming down into this cellar neither."

"Nobody's goin' to come down here," C. J. countered. By this time it was obvious that he was irritated with his companion. "Come on, Monte! We've got to get these boxes in the tunnel and get a lock fixed on the trapdoor, so let's get with it. OK?"

Monte was still complaining as their footsteps creaked up the stairs and ceased suddenly.

"They're coming back any minute!" Kevin exclaimed. "And when they do, they're going to

open the trapdoor and we'll be had! We've got
to get out of here!"

"If there's any place to go!" Hip cried. By this
time Kevin wasn't the only one who was
frightened.

"This is a tunnel that leads to an old cave,"
Hank said. "Arden Nitler and Scott Merrill and
I found it a couple of years ago. Come on. We
can go back so far they'll never find us."

Hank led the boys 75 or 100 feet away from
the entrance, beyond the place where the man-
made tunnel joined the cave. The only difference
that Greg could see was that the man-made
tunnel or shaft was supported by old timbers,
indicating that it had been cut through loose
clay or shale. But the walls of the cave were
hard and rough.

"There," Hank said, keeping his voice to a
whisper. "That ought to be far enough."

One of the other boys started to speak but
stopped as they heard something heavy being
set down on the floor of the tunnel. The sound
carried along the long, narrow corridor so
clearly that Greg shuddered. It was almost as
though C. J. and Monte were within half a dozen
feet of them.

"Watch it, Monte!" the taller man cried in
warning. "That stuff is breakable, you know."

"OK. If you don't like the way I'm doin' it,
you can get in here and do anything you want
to."

"Shut up!"

Bernard Palmer

The kids counted the boxes being placed in the tunnel. One—two—three—four—five. When the last was in place Monte grunted his satisfaction. "There, that's done! And I didn't break nothin'!"

"It's a wonder," his companion muttered. "Now, get out of there and get this hasp and padlock in place. We've got other things to do."

A moment later the voices were blocked out by the sound of a battery-operated drill cutting bolt holes in the heavy trapdoor in order to fasten the hasp in place.

"Now," Kevin said, his voice breaking dangerously, "we're in a worse mess than ever. Those guys are fixin' such a big lock on that door we won't be able to get it open. We'll starve down here."

"We don't have to get out that way," Hank told him calmly. "This cave leads up the mountain to the place where the old Oriental mansion used to be—the one that burned down. We can go up there and get out."

"Isn't that sort of strange?" Greg asked. "That mansion is at the cave entrance and the Oriental store is at the other end—at the tunnel entrance. Quite a coincidence, isn't it?"

"Not the way I look at it," the other boy said. "I figure they built the mansion up there because they had found the cave and knew that it led down the mountain to a place close to the store. All they had to do was dig a short tunnel connecting the two and they could go back and forth whenever they wanted to without anybody knowing it."

Greg thought about that for a time, as the boys picked their way through the debris in the tunnel toward the mountain.

"It sounds logical," Hip put in. "And that's pretty smart, too. They could hide stuff in the tunnel and the chances were that no one would know anything about it. They could even go from the mansion to the store and back again without being seen."

"What I can't figure out is, how did C. J. and Monte find out about it?" Kevin wanted to know.

"They may have gone exploring, the way Arden and Scott and I did," Hank told him. "Or, somebody may have mentioned it to them. I'm sure there are quite a few people who know about it."

"Well," Hip said, changing the subject abruptly. "We found out a couple of things this morning."

"That Monte and C. J. know about the tunnel is one," Kevin put in. "What's the other one?"

"I wasn't even thinking about that. I was thinking about the stuff they put in the tunnel. We found out that they aren't looking for something. They're hiding something."

"That's right!" Greg exclaimed.

"Maybe they robbed a bank," Kevin said, "and are hiding the loot down in the tunnel."

"No, it can't be that," Hip continued. "Whatever it is that they hid, it's breakable. We heard C. J. say so."

"It doesn't make sense," Hank said aloud.

"It would probably make a lot of sense if we could unravel the rest of the mystery," Greg answered.

"That's right." Determination crept into Hank's voice. "It would help a lot if we just knew what those guys hid down there."

"We could go back and take a look," Greg said, straightening slowly and blinking in the sunlight.

"Greg, are you out of your ever-lovin' mind?" Kevin exclaimed.

"Monte and C. J. are long gone," Hank added. "There's nothing to be afraid of."

"You hope."

"M-Maybe they knew we were in there and pretended like they'd gone so we'd come back to that end of the tunnel where they could grab us," Kevin told them.

"No way," Hank replied. "If they knew we were here they'd have come barrelin' after us."

"OK," Greg said, stopping the discussion abruptly. "We take a vote. How many want to go back with Hank and me to see what's in those boxes?"

"I do," Hip said.

"How about you, Kev?"

"I vote 'no.' "

"Then you can stay here and wait for us."

The three boys started back down the steep, sloping cave, single file.

"Hey, you guys!" Kevin called out, hurrying after them. "You can't leave me alone!"

At first it seemed to the boys that they had gone several blocks back into the mountain, but in a couple of minutes they were at the mouth of the tunnel. The faint, wavering beam of the flashlight picked out the dark forms of the wooden crates that C. J. and Monte had left there.

"Wow!" Kevin exclaimed. "Look at the size of them!"

"It's what's in 'em that counts," Hip reminded him.

They crouched around the nearest box, staring at it. "They're all nailed shut," Greg said softly.

Hank took the flashlight from Greg's hand and probed the floor of the tunnel until he found a rock twice the size of his fist. "We can use this as a hammer," he said.

Kevin shifted his weight nervously from one leg to the other. "I hope those dudes don't decide to come back down in the cellar about now," he said, more to himself than the others.

In an instant or two Hank had two boards off the crate and held the light close, revealing some neatly folded newsprint covered with characters from an Oriental language.

"What a bummer!" he moaned.

"There's got to be something else in there," Greg said.

Hank reached in and fumbled around until his fingers discovered a small object wrapped in newspaper.

"What's this?" he mumbled.

Greg didn't know what he expected, but he groaned aloud as he saw a small, delicate porcelain figure of an Oriental woman sharply outlined in the beam of the flashlight.

"Man," Hip exclaimed. "What do they want with that?"

"Search me," Greg replied. He reached in and unwrapped another object—a vase 8 or 10 inches high.

"Well, I sure wouldn't give them much for that," Kevin observed.

Greg had to admit that the items they had seen in the box so far didn't look like very much to him either, but there were probably many people who would give a lot for it. That had to be the reason C. J. and Monte went to all the trouble of buying those old buildings—just to have a good place to hide those boxes. Although that didn't really make sense, either.

"Do you suppose they stole this stuff?" Kevin asked.

"Could be."

"Then we'd better get out of here! They might be back any time! You never know what a couple of guys like that will do!"

"I suppose you're right about getting out of here," Greg admitted, "but I want to get some pictures first."

He set the two objects on the crate and snapped several closeups. The boys jumped as his flash went off.

"That ought to be enough, hadn't it?" his brother asked nervously.

"I think I've got a couple more exposures left in this pack." Greg backed up and took a shot of all five boxes.

"There!" he said. "That winds it up. I don't have any more film."

"That's the best news I've heard all day," Kevin retorted.

The boys turned and made their way through the tunnel to the cave, up to the entrance behind the ruins of the old burned-down mansion.

"Man!" Kevin exclaimed, "doesn't the sun look bright and friendly? I was beginnning to wonder if we'd ever see it again!"

11

Once the boys were out of the cave Greg laid his pictures on a rock and let them develop. Kevin made a remark about hanging around a place where C. J. and Monte were apt to come, and how foolish it was; however, he was as interested in the photographs as his companions.

At first the prints were fuzzy and indistinct. Then vague outlines of the objects Greg photographed took shape—the square of the wooden crate, with the small figurine and the vase on top. The inky blackness of the tunnel swallowed the rest of the flash and the color of the print was poor. The figurine and the vase were distinct, but he had been too far away to bring out the detail.

The closeups were much better. They could see the fine lines of the woman's hair in the figurine. Her eyes were smaller than pinheads yet amazingly expressive, and her features were exquisitely cut. The boys realized that, whoever she was, she must have been beautiful.

The vase had pleasing lines and was covered with an intricate design that was distinctly Oriental. The color in the print wasn't as true as Greg would have liked to have it, but there was enough there to indicate what the vase actually looked like.

"That stuff is sort of neat, isn't it?" Greg observed.

Hank nodded. "Not neat enough to go to the trouble those guys have gone to, though."

"Unless it's worth a lot of money," Hip said.

Greg picked up the pictures and, with a final look, returned them to his shirt pocket.

"I think we ought to tell Dad about all this stuff in the tunnel," Kevin said. "He can go to the sheriff and have him arrest C. J. and Monte."

Greg's forehead corrugated. "It's sure something to think about," he replied uncertainly. "Only—"

"Only what?"

"Only we've got to be sure that C. J. and Monte stole those things first."

"After what they said a little while ago?" Kevin exploded. "They practically admitted that they stole it."

The older boy did not answer him.

When the foursome got back to the motor home, Mr. and Mrs. Powell, Kim and Somi were just pulling in beside it. Relief was evident in the tiny Oriental girl's face as she got out of the truck. Greg knew, even before he asked, that Wai Chun Hing was better. Kim verified his observation before he even asked about the sick man.

". . . and we're so happy that he's feeling better!" she said.

"He's still sick," Somi reminded Kim. "And he hurts something terrible . . . "

"But the doctor says that he thinks he is going to be all right," Kim added.

"That's great," Greg exclaimed. "We've been praying for him."

Bernard Palmer

Questions leaped to Somi's eyes, but instead of asking them, she thanked him gratefully. It was obvious that she didn't quite know what he meant but she appreciated any kind of help from anywhere.

The boys followed Mr. and Mrs. Powell and the girls into the motor home where Christine elaborated on the information Kim had just given them.

"The doctor diagnosed Wai Chun Hing's difficulty as an aggravation of his arthritis," she said, "but it is not serious."

"Good," Hip said.

"Still, he'll have to be in the hospital for a week or so."

"And Somi's going to stay with us," Kimberly put in.

Mrs. Powell went on to explain that the doctor suggested she phone the elderly man's daughter, who lives in San Francisco. "He didn't think there was anything to be alarmed about, but thought she ought to know. She was very concerned when I talked with her, and she's going to fly out as soon as she can."

There was so much excitement about Wai Chun Hing and his illness and the fact that his only child was coming to see him that Greg and his friends temporarily forgot about the Oriental art objects and the secret tunnel where they were hidden. Mr. Powell reminded them, however, when he took the newspaper from a nearby table and opened it to an inside page.

100

"I bought this paper in town this morning. I want you guys to read something."

Greg took the current copy of the *Denver Post* and read: "C. J. Larreau and Monte Grimm, who recently purchased property in Poor Boy's Folly with a view to opening a dude ranch in that well-known ghost town west of Denver announced today that they had made an exciting find of Oriental artifacts in one of the buildings. They said they had withheld announcement of the discovery until representative pieces of the find could be examined and authenticated by Dr. J. William Prentice, an internationally known authority on Oriental art.

"In Dr. Prentice's considered opinion, the pieces are genuine and have probably been in the area since the silver rush when multitudes of laborers were brought over from the Orient to work the mines. 'The tongs were very active in the Poor Boy area,' the scientist said. 'I am of the opinion that the items discovered by Mr. Larreau and Mr. Grimm make up at least part of the treasury of one of those tongs. How it escaped discovery for so many years remains a mystery . . . .' "

The boys looked at one another, questions standing full in their eyes. What this Dr. Prentice said sounded convincing enough, Greg told himself, but it didn't square with the facts as he and his pals knew them. C. J. and Monte hadn't found the stuff in the ghost town. They had stashed it there, after getting it from somewhere else. That much they knew for sure.

"Do you believe that story, Dad?" Greg asked.

"I don't have any reason not to believe it," Mr. Powell replied. "It makes sense in spite of the fact that it seems strange no one has found it until now.

"My research turned up stories of tong wars in Poor Boy's Folly, so we know that part is true. And it is a well-known fact that the tongs had treasuries of considerable value. If they were afraid another tong was out to steal their wealth, they just might hide it well enough so it would take all this time to locate it." He nodded thoughtfully. "Yes, the things those men found could very well be part of one of those treasuries."

"We figured they stole 'em," Kevin put in.

His dad's head came up quickly. "We?"

Greg could see the color creep into his younger brother's cheeks and the wheels of his mind turn as he realized how close he was to giving away their secret.

"But what you say sounds reasonable," Kevin finished lamely.

Greg noted that he hadn't actually lied, but he had been close to it.

The boys went outside after a few minutes. When they were far enough away from the motor home to be sure they would not be overheard Greg took the Polaroid pictures from his pocket and studied them again.

"I wish we could get to the hospital and see Wai Chun Hing," he said. "He might be able to tell us something about the stuff just by looking at the pictures."

"What's to tell?" Hank asked. "They're just ordinary pictures, and not very good ones at that."

The light dimmed in Greg's eyes. "It was just a thought," he muttered. "I figured maybe he could look at the pictures and tell us whether or not he thought those things were genuine." He paused significantly. "I've got a hunch they aren't real."

"I don't know anything about this stuff," Hank put in, "but I don't think he's going to be able to tell us what we want to know by looking at a picture . . . If we want to get anything out of Wai Chun Hing, we'll have to get him the real thing."

Greg's eyelids narrowed. "What do you mean?"

"We'll have to show him one of those pieces we looked at," Hank explained.

Slowly Greg began to understand what his pal was suggesting. "We can't do that. It would be stealing!"

"I don't see how you figure that. We wouldn't figure on taking it. We'd just 'borrow' it for a couple of days."

"No way," Greg retorted emphatically.

"Then we'll never find out the truth," Hank said in disgust. "It's as simple as that."

That evening after supper and devotions the guys were playing catch when a woman arrived in a rented car. She wheeled into the little clearing, slammed on the brakes and got out.

Greg and his companions stared at her. She was shorter than Mrs. Powell by at least four inches; a slight, smartly dressed Oriental woman who looked as though she had miraculously appeared from the full color pages of a fashion magazine. Her shoes, gloves and purse matched the soft shade of her dress and her shining black hair was strikingly styled.

For a moment she remained at the car, her hand on the still-open door. "Is this the Powell residence?" she asked, a slight, superior slur in her voice.

"You must be Wai Chun Hing's daughter," Greg said.

She nodded, stiffening to indicate she did not appreciate such familiarity. "I am Mrs. Lee Kee," she informed him as though he was supposed to recognize the name. "Is—are your parents at home?"

By this time Mrs. Powell was standing at the door of the motor home, smiling warmly. "You must be Leslie," she said, drying her hands on the hem of her apron. "Your father has been speaking of you often."

This time Mrs. Kee ignored the familiarity. "I would like to talk with you privately," she said. "May I come in?"

"Of course." Christine Powell stood to one side and held the door open for her guest. "Would you like some tea?"

"I'm afraid I won't be able to take time for that," she answered. "I really must be getting back to the hospital. But there is something I must talk to you about." She grimaced as she saw that the kids were standing near the door listening.

Mrs. Powell saw her look of displeasure. "Greg," she said, "why don't you and your friends go down to the creek, OK?"

"Sure. Come on, guys."

They left, but not before they heard Mrs. Kee ask, "Who is this *Somi* Father mentions so often?" There was a sharp edge to her voice.

"Wow!" Kevin exclaimed. "She's really something!"

"You can say that again," Hank replied. "She's been back here before a few times. Drives a neat Mercedes that must've cost 25 or 30 thou. Dad says she married a rich Oriental merchant in California and comes back every once in awhile trying to talk her father into moving out there to live with her."

"I can see why he wouldn't want to," Hip replied. "Just listening to her for an hour could give a guy the stomachache."

The boys hadn't been down to the creek more than four or five minutes when the door opened and Mrs. Kee came out. She stepped from the motor home gingerly and turned to Mrs. Powell.

"Father says you and your husband came out to see him after this—this Somi person came and told you that he was ill, and you saw that he got to the hospital," she was saying.

"We were glad to be able to help," Christine Powell told her.

"I would like to pay you for what you did."

"Oh, no," she answered quickly. "We couldn't take anything."

Mrs. Kee seemed baffled—unable to understand why Mrs. Powell spoke as she had. She started fumbling uncertainly in her purse. "But you incurred some expense in driving down to Father's and then back to the store to phone the hospital. And you made two trips to town and had a long distance call to me in San Francisco."

She extracted a hundred dollar bill from her purse. "I would like to pay you."

"Thank you, no." Mrs. Powell was kindly but firm in her refusal. "We wouldn't hear of it. We love your father and Somi."

"Somi!" Mrs. Kee's lips curled contemptuously about the word.

12

Hank Wendland was at the Powell motor home early the following morning as usual. He squatted on the ground and leaned against a slender aspen while waiting for Greg and Hip to come out.

"Hi," he said as they appeared. "Goin' to the hospital?"

Greg shook his head. "Dad was going," he said, "but changed his mind after Wai Chun Hing's daughter showed up. He isn't sure she wants us to be around her father."

"She's somethin' else." A wistful tone crept into Hank's voice. "I wish she'd offered me that hundred bucks. I'd have taken it."

"Me, too," Hip replied.

They left the motor home and sauntered toward the trail that led up the mountain to the ghost town. Nobody had said anything about going back there. They had just begun to move in that direction, automatically.

"What's she going to do about Somi?" Hank wanted to know.

Greg shrugged.

"I don't think she likes her."

"That's for sure," Hip added. "You heard how she said her name, didn't you?"

"The only thing she talked about to Mom was the fact that her father was getting older and was no longer able to take care of himself. She didn't care what he said, she was going to take

Bernard Palmer

him home with her as soon as he was released
from the hospital and able to travel."

"Poor guy," Kevin murmured. "She's his own
daughter. He'll have to put up with her."

"Yeah." And then Greg thought about Somi—
the shy, sensitive little girl who had been living
with Wai Chun Hing. "I know someone who'll
have to put up with her, too. And it'll be even
harder for her than it will for the old man."

His companions nodded in agreement. "It's
going to be a bummer for Somi," Hip said.

"Maybe Wai Chun Hing won't go to San Francisco, after all," Hank put in. "Maybe he'll tell
her to pack it in."

There was a long silence.

"I wish we could get to the hospital to see
him for a few minutes," Greg said presently. "He
might be a big help to us in figuring out what
C. J. and Monte are up to." The thought excited
him.

"You know, he might be able to tell us whether
he thinks that stuff could have come from here
like those dudes say or if they brought it in
from somewhere like we think they did."

"Maybe." Hank glanced obliquely at his companions. "I just happened to remember that
Dad's going to town this afternoon. We could
ride along—" he paused significantly, "that is if
we had some reason for going—like having
something to show Wai Chun Hing."

"What about the pictures I took?"

Hank's nose wrinkled. "A lot of good that
would do."

Greg understood what his friend was hinting at and his lithe young body stiffened. "I've already told you," he retorted, "we're not going to steal one of those pieces to show to him."

"For cryin' out loud! It wouldn't be stealing!"

"I don't know what else you would call it."

"We'd just be borrowing it for a day or two. Besides, we know C. J. and Monte are crooks. How can you steal from dudes like that?"

When Hank explained it that way Greg began to wonder if his friend was right. After all, he reasoned, they wouldn't be taking the pieces of art for themselves. They would only be doing it to show Wai Chun Hing in order to see if he believed it was genuine or not. And if he did, to see if he recognized it as anything he had seen in the ghost town when he was young.

"We're not going to steal anything," Hank repeated. "You ought to know me well enough by now to believe that. I'm not a thief."

Greg nodded. Hank hadn't received Christ as his Saviour, but he was a good guy. He didn't steal or get into trouble.

"We'll just take a couple of pieces long enough to take them to the hospital to show old Wai Chun Hing."

"What if C. J. and Monte come back before we can return the stuff?"

"We'll nail the boards back on the crate. They'll never know the difference." Hank evaded the question. He grasped Greg's arm. "How about it?"

"Well—"

"Good!" Hank took the reluctant word as an indication of agreement. "Get your flashlight and let's move it. We've got to hurry or we won't be back in time to go to the hospital with Dad."

"Wait a minute," Greg countered. "Who said anything about going down in that cave?"

"You did—just now."

"I—" He really didn't want to go but he could not think of any logical arguments to counter Hank's pressure. He looked over at Hip for support but his Chicano friend didn't say anything.

"I know where your flashlight is," Hank went on. "I'll get it."

Moments later they were on the trail up to the ruins of the old mansion. Greg's feet dragged and the uneasiness within him grew with each step closer to the cave and the Oriental artifacts.

All the things Hank said were true, he reasoned. They weren't going to take anything for themselves. In fact, he didn't even like the looks of the pieces they had dug out of the crate. At least not well enough to take them. They were just going to show a couple of them to Wai Chun Hing and then return them. That wouldn't be stealing. *Or would it?*

Greg's dad had always taught him that he should never take anything that belonged to someone else, for any reason. It didn't make any difference how large or how small it was, or why he felt he should.

"The Bible says, 'Thou shalt not steal,' " Mr. Powell had always said. "There are no exceptions." According to that definition, Greg's nagging heart told him this was stealing.

Yet they did have a good motive for taking a couple of pieces for a little while—and Hank was so positive there was nothing wrong with it that Greg was confused. Neither Hip nor Kevin had protested either, so they must approve.

Greg almost hoped they would see C. J.'s car parked near the cave entrance—or that they would at least find tire tracks that would indicate the two men had been there recently. Either would give him an excuse for refusing to go into the cave for the artifacts. However, there was no sign that anyone had been within miles of the place in months. Even the brush at the mouth of the cave looked as though it had not been molested.

"Well," Hank said, taking the flashlight in his right hand. "Here we are."

Once more Greg hesitated. "Do—do you really think we ought to do this?"

His friend glared at him. "Now don't start that again!" he muttered contemptuously.

Hank parted the brush with care to avoid breaking any branches, and Greg and the other two followed him into the cave, single file. The beam of the flashlight pushed the darkness to either side, revealing the dank, musty floor that led into the mountain 30 or 40 feet before turning sharply to plunge downward. It fell away much more steeply than Greg had remembered. They seemed propelled toward the tunnel and the dread thing they were going to do. By now Greg was sure that he and Hip and Kevin should be having no part in the project.

"Hank," he exclaimed suddenly with a firmness that surprised himself.

The leader stopped and turned, shining the light in his direction. "Now what?"

"This is wrong. I'm not going to do it and I don't think Hip and Kevin ought to either."

Hank groaned audibly. "Hey, man, come on! I suppose it's that religion of yours that's bothering you!"

"It's not the kind of thing a Christian ought to do—if that's what you mean." Greg took a deep breath. "I should never have let you talk me into it. I knew better. But I was so anxious to find out what's at the bottom of this mystery I went along with you."

Hank sensed that it was useless to argue. "Well," he grated angrily, "you can go back if you want to but I'm goin' on! I'll get a couple of those pieces just like we planned and I'll see Wai Chun Hing! If you want to be such dopes, OK, but you're not gettin' me to go along with it! That's for sure."

"We can't make you go back with us," Greg said, "but we wish you would."

"Yeah," Hip put in. "There're other ways we can find out what Monte and C. J. are up to."

"Like what?"

He fell silent.

"I'm not givin' you your flashlight either," Hank said. "You'll have to find your way back in the dark."

Greg was surprised at how good he felt now that he had decided to turn away from Hank's plan. "We can manage," he said. "Come on guys."

Before they could move Hank continued, angrily, "You'd better not tell anybody about this if you know what's good for you."

"We're not going to lie about it," Greg answered, "if that's what you mean."

"They'll never do anything to me, anyway," the other boy retorted. "Not for taking something from C. J. and Monte."

"Come on," Greg said, ignoring Hank's protests.

The three of them had covered perhaps 50 or 60 feet, feeling their way along in the darkness, when they heard the sound of running behind them and saw the bobbing flashlight beam. Hank was hurrying to catch up with them.

"You guys make me sick," he muttered as he slowed to walk with Greg and his companions. "If you weren't so stupid we'd have that stuff right now and be on our way back out with it."

They left the cave and made their way down the steep path to Poor Boy's Folly. At first Hank's lips curled bitterly and he refused to talk to anyone, but as they entered the ghost town his pouting lips began to relax.

"Wonder if those dudes are here today?" he asked.

Kevin shuddered.

Hank acted as though he was about to say more but stopped suddenly and glanced at his watch. "I've got to split or I won't get to go with Dad." He turned from his companions. "I'll be seeing you."

"Hey!" Greg called after him. "My flashlight!"

But Hank acted as though he hadn't heard him.

Greg, Hip and Kevin continued through the ghost town where they soon discovered that the story about C. J. and Monte buying some of the deserted buildings was true. There were heavy padlocks on the doors of the hotel, the store and the two structures between. Each sported huge signs: "PRIVATE PROPERTY. NO TRESPASSING. VIOLATORS WILL BE PROSECUTED."

"Know what I think?" Hip muttered, chuckling.

"I didn't know you ever did any thinking," Greg said.

"Well, I do. Every once in awhile." He pulled his slight form erect. "I don't believe those guys want us snooping around."

They walked slowly down the narrow boardwalk, studying the hard-packed road that ran the length of the ghost town for some sign of a vehicle having been parked there. However, they saw nothing that would indicate anyone had been there since the boys were trapped in the cellar and almost caught by C. J. and Monte.

"Let's go 'round in back," Kevin said at last, curiosity tinging his voice.

They went beyond the last NO TRESPASSING sign to a narrow passageway between two buildings and ended up in the alley where C. J.'s car had been parked.

"There's no sign of that car here now," Kevin said.

"You didn't expect to see it, did you?" Hip asked.

The younger boy laughed nervously. "I don't know what to expect."

Hip went briskly to the place where the car had stood and began to examine the ground. "Those dudes have been back," he announced. "These tracks are fresh."

Greg had to agree. "They were probably here last night."

"Or maybe this morning," Kevin answered. "They might even have been in that tunnel when Hank wanted us to go down there. I'm sure glad you changed our minds, Greg."

"Me, too," Hip added.

Greg paused long enough to look up. "I'm sure not very proud of the way I handled it," he said. "I almost let him talk me into doing something I knew a Christian—or anyone else, for that matter—had no business doing."

"But he made it sound so innocent and logical," Kevin said.

"And I almost fell for it."

"Anyway," Hip muttered, "I'm glad we didn't go any farther than we did."

Greg started to speak but something caught his eye. He stooped quickly and picked up a fragment of old newspaper. "Take a squint at this, will you?"

Hip took it from him. "I suppose you expect me to read it?"

"Why not?" Greg said, laughing. "It's only in Chinese or Japanese or something like it."

"Hey!" his Chicano friend exclaimed. "Know what? That looks like one of the papers that stuff in the tunnel was wrapped in."

The boys stared at the crumpled piece of old newspaper with the picture of a dignified elderly military officer on it.

"I think you're right," Greg said.

"What do you s'pose that means?" Kevin wanted to know. "Have they hauled that stuff out again?"

Hip's lips tightened. "Maybe they dropped this when they took the boxes inside."

"They couldn't have," Greg countered. "Those crates were nailed shut. Remember?"

His companions nodded.

"But how did it get out here?" Hip asked Greg. "It's been a long time since any Orientals have lived here in Poor Boy's Folly."

"Maybe I'm right," Kevin said. "They might have changed their minds and taken the stuff out of here."

"That doesn't make any sense, either," Greg replied. "They wouldn't go to all the trouble they've gone to, then change their minds."

13

At supper that night Greg could think of little more than the art pieces, C. J. and Monte, and the piece of crumpled newspaper in his shirt pocket. It would have been strange enough finding a quarter of a sheet of the *Denver Post* or the *Rocky Mountain News* behind a store building in a ghost town where nobody, except old Mr. Heskett, lived. But a piece of foreign newsprint was absolutely bewildering.

The paper had been dropped recently, probably within the last day or two because it had rained hard the week before, and rain would have ruined it. But what was a foreign newspaper doing in Poor Boy's Folly where no Orientals had lived for years? It had to be tied in with the boxes of art pieces, somehow.

The stuff had been packed in newspaper just like that. But, as Hip said, the crates had been tightly closed when the kids saw them and they had closed the one they opened, so the paper had to have gotten out in the alley some other way. Perhaps C. J. and Monte had repacked the boxes, for some reason—or taken them out and disposed of them.

Greg was still pondering the mystery when his dad reached for the Bible and handed it to Kim. She read a portion of the New Testament. Before they prayed, Mrs. Powell had a request.

"We should be praying for Wai Chun Hing," she began.

"I thought he was getting along OK," Kevin was curious.

"He's supposed to get out of the hospital in a few days," Somi told him.

Greg waited with growing uneasiness. He knew his mother well enough to know that she was deeply disturbed. He caught it in her voice and saw it in her eyes.

"Mrs. Kee—his daughter—says that she is going to take him to California with her."

"That might be best for him," Mr. Powell replied. "He's going to have trouble taking care of himself for awhile."

"Yes," Christine answered. She glanced significantly at Somi, "but—"

Tears ran down Somi's cheeks. "I already know," she said. "Mrs. Kee told me today that she was going to see the county social worker to have her find a place for me to stay."

"That's not going to happen," George Powell said sternly.

"B-B-But it is. Mrs. Kee said that Grandfather doesn't need me any more. He has his own grandchildren."

"We're still not going to let that happen," Mr. Powell repeated.

Hope glimmered in the girl's eyes. Then it died slowly. "She'll never change. *I know it!*"

"Why don't we pray about it and trust God to do what's best for everybody. OK?"

She nodded but it was obvious that she had no confidence in prayer. That night after everyone had gone to bed Greg heard Somi's muffled sobbing and Kim's whispered efforts to comfort her.

The next morning when Somi got up her eyes were red and swollen. She had little to say to anyone. Greg knew how badly she must feel and his heart ached for her, but there was nothing he could do to help. He didn't know whether there was anything anyone could do, except to pray.

That morning the Powells had just finished breakfast when Hank showed up again—as he always seemed to do. Greg recognized his excited knock on the door and went to open it. He thought his friend might still be irritated because he had refused to go down the tunnel and take a couple of those pieces from the boxes C. J. and Monte had put there. However, there was no sign of anger on the other boy's face. It looked to Greg as though Hank had completely forgotten the incident.

"Have you seen yesterday's *Denver Post*?" Hank opened the paper and thrust it into Greg's hands.

"What's that?" Mr. Powell called from inside the motor home.

"A story about the big auction up here next week."

"That can't be."

The Wendland boy stepped inside with Greg. "There is going to be another auction—of some Oriental stuff those two dudes, C. J. and Monte, found in one of the buildings."

Greg sat down in the captain's chair just inside the motor home door and read the account aloud. Now that the authorities were convinced the pieces were genuine antiques, the men who discovered them were going to hold an auction the following Friday, beginning at 12 noon, the story said. An ad on the next page explained that C. J. and Monte were moving to Poor Boy's Folly immediately and would be showing the items to interested buyers. It would also be possible to make direct purchases before the sale.

"Well," Mr. Powell said when Greg had finished reading, "with two auctions in one month this is getting to be a popular place."

"That's what my dad says," Hank replied.

Greg studied his father's lean face. If he suspected there was anything wrong with the art objects or the sale, he was careful to keep from showing it. Finally Greg could contain himself no longer. "Are you going up to the hotel to interview them?"

Mr. Powell shook his head.

"You'll be getting some pictures, won't you?"

"We'll have to see about that a little later. Today I'm going up to the courthouse to see the social worker."

Somi, who was standing beside Kim, looked away quickly. Greg was sure that she was about to start crying again.

Usually Greg and the boys didn't hang around the motor home long when Hank came over. They always tried to get away from the girls and Kevin if they could. But this day they didn't feel like tearing off. For one thing, Greg wasn't too anxious to go up to the ghost town and he didn't think Hip or Hank really wanted to go prowling around up there now that C. J. and Monte were probably living in one of those buildings. For another, Greg was concerned about Somi. She looked so miserable he didn't like leaving her and Kim alone.

"Want to go fishing?" he asked her and his sister.

Somi shook her head.

"How about a hike and a picnic?"

"You go ahead." She forced a thin, crooked smile. "I think I'll just wait here until your father comes back."

"We could go on a picnic and be back here before he's home," Kim put in. "He'll go to the hospital to see your grandfather and everything."

Still Somi shook her head, her expression unchanged. "I don't feel like a picnic. If you want to, go on. It won't make me feel bad."

"I'll stay here, too," Kim said quickly.

"Let's all stick around," Hip said. "We can have as much fun here as we can on a picnic."

It was mid-afternoon when Mr. Powell came back. Greg read the concern on his usually mild features as he got out of the pickup and headed for the house. Somi approached him hesitantly. "Did you talk to the—the lady at the courthouse?"

He nodded. "She's been in touch with your aunt by phone and is going to try to get her to come back here so she can talk to her in person," he said.

Somi's cheeks were sallow and her lips quivered. "I—I'm not going to get to stay with Grandfather, am I?" she asked.

Mr. Powell flashed the grin he usually reserved for Kim and rumpled her hair with a big, calloused hand.

"We'll have to see about that." He started into the motor home, but with his hand on the door, he turned back to her. "I do have some good news for you. Your grandfather was released from the hospital today."

Her features brightened. "Where is he? Can I see him?"

"I'll take you over to the house in a few minutes."

Somi glanced quickly at Kim. "I could run over there," she said. "It would be just as quick."

Kim went with her. While they were gone, Mr. Powell called the boys into the house.

"I want to talk to Greg and Kevin and their mother," he told Hank and Hip, "but you can sit in, if you like."

Greg went over to the table and sat near his mother, while Kevin and their two friends found seats at the rear of the motor home. Mr. Powell spun the driver's seat to face the tense little group and sat down.

"Is it about Somi?" Greg asked.

His dad nodded. "Nothing has been decided yet," he said, "but it's obvious that she's not going to get to stay with Wai Chun Hing."

"What about her aunt?" Mrs. Powell asked. "Is her health any better? Could she take her?"

"I'm afraid not," Mr. Powell pulled in a deep breath. "Her health isn't at all good."

"But what's Somi going to do?" Greg wanted to know. "She can't go into any old foster home— just to have someone who's willing to take care of her."

"She could come and live with us," Kevin said.

Greg's eyes widened. "Hey! That sounds neat! I never thought of that!"

Tears flooded Mrs. Powell's eyes.

"That's exactly what I've been hoping to hear," George Powell said. "I've been thinking about it all the way home."

"Can we, Dad?" Kevin cried. "Can we?"

"Now, wait a minute!" Mr. Powell protested. "We don't know if the authorities would permit it, or if Somi would be happy living with us."

"Can I ask her, Dad?" Kevin said, his eyes dancing.

"I don't think we should say anything to her until we've learned what the social worker and Somi's aunt think. They'll have to be satisfied that's the best thing to do."

Before allowing the boys to leave, Mr. and Mrs. Powell extracted a promise from both Hi-polita and Hank that they would say nothing about the proposal until the family had final word from the social worker and the girl's aunt.

"And especially don't say anything to Somi," Mr. Powell cautioned.

"You can count on us," they assured him.

14

Mrs. Powell got the boys some cookies and milk. When they had finished eating and were filing outside, Kim and Somi shuffled back to the motor home, their shoulders sagging and their faces somber.

"How was he?" Greg asked as they approached. It was all he could do to keep from blurting out the news his folks had insisted be kept from Somi.

"We didn't get to see him," Kim said.

"S-S-She said that Grandfather was sleeping," the younger girl explained.

Mrs. Powell opened the door in time to hear what Somi said. "Perhaps he was asleep," she reminded the girls. "He has been very ill and is very weak."

"Maybe," Kim said doubtfully, "and maybe not."

"I'm sure Mrs. Kee will let you see him tomorrow."

"T-That's what she said," the young Thai girl replied, "but I—I don't know if she will or not."

"I think we have to believe what she tells us, don't you?" Mrs. Powell asked. "At least until we know for sure that she is telling us something that isn't true."

Somi nodded uncertainly.

Greg went over to her, impulsively. Somehow even the possibility that she might come to live with them changed his attitude toward her. He felt protective, the way he did with Kim.

"You'll get to see your grandfather," he said firmly.

"That's what everybody says," she told him without conviction.

"You'll see," he repeated. "If she won't let you, Dad'll take you over there. He'll get you in the house."

She wiped a tear away.

His lips parted, but he caught himself just in time to keep from telling her what his dad had made him promise not to. He didn't know it would be so hard to keep quiet—especially when she was so worried and everything.

She saw that he was about to speak and waited expectantly. He hadn't intended to show her the scrap of newsprint in his shirt pocket, but it was the only thing he could think of to talk about right then.

"Can you read this?" he questioned, taking the folded paper from his pocket and handing it to her.

She saw at a glance that it was written in Chinese characters and shook her head. "Grandfather was beginning to teach me character writing when he got sick, but I've never learned enough of it to read more than my name." She was about to hand the paper back when she caught a glimpse of the picture on the back.

"I've seen that picture before lots of times," she exclaimed excitedly. "Grandfather has a big one just like this, only in color, hanging on the wall of his bedroom."

"Who is it?" Greg asked.

"All he ever told me was that it was a picture of one of the greatest Chinese generals who had ever lived."

Greg was somewhat disappointed as he shoved it back in his pocket. When she got so excited he thought she might have some information that was helpful to him and his pals in unraveling the mystery.

The next morning Mr. Powell suggested to Somi that he take her and Kim down to the old man's home. When they got there Mrs. Kee was in the yard, watering the flowers. She frowned her disapproval but allowed the girls to go in and talk to Wai Chun Hing.

As soon as they were in the house and the door had closed behind them, George told Mrs. Kee of his family's hope to take Somi as their daughter.

"I am concerned about the girl's welfare, of course," she said coldly, "but she is no relation of mine."

"Perhaps not," he explained, "but I would like to have you talk it over with your father."

Anger flashed hotly in her dark cheeks. "I would rather you not talk with Father about her."

"But she means a great deal to him," Mr. Powell said. "I feel that he should be consulted."

"Father has been so ill that I—I haven't said anything to him about—about our plans for Somi," she went on. "I'm afraid it will upset him at a time when he should not be upset."

Mr. Powell hesitated briefly, then thanked her and left. "I felt like telling her that her father is of age and so am I," he said to Greg and his wife later, "and that I would talk with Wai Chun Hing when and where I felt like, but I didn't. I might have to confront her, but I don't want to unless that is the only alternative."

At first Greg and his friends didn't think much about the fact that old Wai Chun Hing had a picture on his wall just like the one on the scrap of newspaper they had found on the ground behind the store. Then they got to thinking about it and finally Hip said that it might be helpful to get him to read the paper and give them a rough translation.

"What good is that?" Hank wanted to know.

"If that stuff was wrapped in newspapers before C. J. and Monte got it," Hip said, "whoever wrapped it would probably pick up the papers they could get their hands on easiest. And that would be those that were printed close by." He grinned impishly. "Want me to draw a picture for you?"

"I think you've got something, Hip," Hank put in.

The next morning the four boys went to see the old Oriental but Mrs. Kee wouldn't let them in.

"We only want to talk to him for a minute or two," Greg protested.

"I don't want him disturbed," she replied icily. "Now, if you'll excuse me, I'm busy." She retreated behind the door and closed it.

The boys came back the next day and the next with the same result. Mrs. Kee met them at the door and refused them admittance.

"I know you think I'm cruel and mean," she said the day before the auction when they came once more. "But I love my father and he's so terribly upset about not being able to take that little girl back to San Francisco with us that I'm afraid he'll be sick again. I don't want anyone to talk with him about her."

"We didn't want to talk about Somi," Hank said quickly. "We've got something else to—to go over with him."

"Are you sure?"

"Positive."

She hesitated uneasily. "You aren't—aren't a Powell, are you?"

"Nope."

"Neither am I," Hip put in.

"All right," she said. "If you'll promise to stop bothering us if you get to talk to him, I'll let you two go in for five minutes."

"Just the two of us?" Hip asked.

"You should be able to talk to Father without upsetting him like someone by the name of Powell might," she said, tears standing in her eyes. "I know you won't start pressuring me or asking him what he wants done about the girl."

Greg didn't want to remain outside, but he had no choice. He and Kevin walked to the edge of the clearing and waited. After a few minutes their companions came out of the house. Mrs.

Kee followed them to the door and thanked them for doing as she had asked them to.

"It wasn't easy," Hip called over his shoulder as he walked away.

Greg and Kevin didn't question their friends until they were well into the forest on the way to the motor home.

"Well," Greg said at last, "how about it?"

"The picture is of some guy by the name of Generalissimo Chiang Kai-shek," Hip said. "I guess he died or was sick or won a war or something to get his picture in the paper."

"Chiang Kai-shek," Greg repeated. "I've heard of him."

"What about the newspaper?" Kevin burst in. "What'd it say?"

"We didn't find out," Hank said. "Wai Chun Hing couldn't find his glasses."

"But we left it there for him," Hip added. "We can go over and see him in the morning and he'll tell us all about it."

"If she'll let us see him," Kevin countered.

"You might not get in," Hip taunted good-naturedly, "but Hank and I are privileged characters."

The Powells had been expecting word from the social worker regarding Somi's getting to stay with them. However they were quite unprepared for the visit that afternoon. Mrs. Powell was just starting supper when a small car drove in beside the motor home and a tall, attractive young woman came to the door.

"I had a phone call from Somi's aunt this afternoon," she began, "and I'm afraid I have bad news for you."

"She's going to be able to keep the girl herself?" Mr. Powell asked.

"No, she won't be able to do that. But she's decided that she wants her raised in a Thai home, if possible."

Greg caught his breath sharply and felt a pain similar to a knife twisting in his heart. Looking over at his parents he knew they were experiencing the same pain.

"But why?" Mrs. Powell asked curiously. "We love Somi and would give her a good home."

The woman across from her squirmed uncomfortably. "I'm convinced of that," she said, "and my report to her was favorable. However she cannot make herself believe that you would treat Somi the same as your own children. She is afraid the difference in race would cause your family and friends to look down on Somi."

"We wouldn't want that, either," Mr. Powell put in quickly. "And if that were the case, we wouldn't even be trying to get her. Is there any way we can convince her that Somi would become our little girl with the same responsibilities and privileges and love the other kids have?"

The social worker shook her head. "She sounded as though her mind is made up when I talked with her this afternoon." She paused for a moment. "If Somi were a ward of the state there would be no question about your getting to take her. However, her aunt is her legal guardian. That means she will have to sign for anyone to adopt her."

They talked for a few minutes and Mrs. Powell walked out to the car with their guest. When she came back there were tears in her eyes.

"I'm glad Somi wasn't here when she came," she said.

"So am I," Mr. Powell replied, "but we will have to tell her, you know . . . Wai Chun Hing and his daughter will be leaving in a couple of days. Before that happens the social workers will have to take Somi to a foster home."

"Couldn't she stay with us until they find a permanent home for her?" Greg asked.

Mr. Powell couldn't answer this question. "We'll have to ask Miss Grainger about it," he said.

The family was more quiet than usual at the table that night, and when the time for prayer came after the Bible reading, Christine had an unspoken request for prayer. Somi looked from one somber face to another with keen discernment.

"What's the matter?" she asked. "Is there something wrong?"

Mr. Powell turned to her. "Mrs. Kee is taking her father to San Francisco in a few days," he said gently.

She nodded.

"Miss Grainger was out this afternoon to tell us that she is looking for a foster home for you."

Somi's face revealed that she didn't quite understand.

"She's finding a place for you to live until she locates a family your aunt approves of."

The girl's lips trembled uncertainly. "Don't *you* want me?"

Mrs. Powell wrapped Somi in her arms and drew her close. "We'd like nothing better than to keep you as our little girl."

She looked up appealingly. "Then why don't you?"

Mr. Powell swallowed against the lump in his throat and Greg saw that there were tears standing in his dad's clear blue eyes. "Your aunt wants you to be raised in a Thai home."

Somi choked back the tears. "Don't I have *any* say about it?"

"Your aunt only wants what she believes is best for you," Christine told her.

"But I don't *want* to live in a Thai home. I told Kim a few days ago that if I couldn't live with Grandfather, I want to live with you."

"Let's pray about it, Dad!" Kevin said suddenly. "God can make Somi's aunt change her mind."

"I'm not going to any other home!" the slight, oval-faced girl exclaimed. "I won't stay! I—I'll run away!"

"Let's talk to God," Mrs. Powell agreed with Kevin. "He cares about our problems."

15

The next morning the Powells had breakfast at the usual time. They tried to pretend that everything was all right, but didn't succeed very well. Conversation came in spurts with long stretches of silence between. And although they tried hard not to keep looking at Somi, they all noticed her swollen, bloodshot eyes.

Greg had pushed the mystery of C. J. and Monte and the Oriental art objects completely out of his mind. He hadn't even remembered that the auction was being held that day, or that Hip and Hank were supposed to go back to see Wai Chun Hing before noon, until his new friend came over to the motor home and reminded them.

"You coming along, Greg?" Hank asked. "Or do you want to wait here?"

Greg got up quickly. "I'll go with you."

"Me, too," Kevin said.

"Nobody asked you."

"That's all right," he answered, slipping into his jacket and starting off with Greg and his friends. "I won't hold that against them."

They were at the edge of the stream when Mr. Powell called them back and suggested they take Somi and Kim along. "She feels so bad," he explained, "that I think it would help her to keep her mind off what is going to happen in a few days."

Neither of the girls acted as though they wanted to walk down the trail to Wai Chun

Hing's house, but when Greg told them the reason for the visit their faces brightened.

"Do you think you'll find out something from Grandfather?" Somi asked.

Greg and Hip shrugged expressively. They could always hope, but that didn't mean they would get any solid information. Now that Greg thought about it, he doubted that talking to the elderly man that morning would clear up much of the mystery. America was full of Orientals and their art. What could they expect to learn from one man?

Nevertheless, they had gone to him with the clipping and he had told them to come back the following morning for a translation. He would be expecting them.

At the edge of the clearing Hip and Hank went ahead to knock on the door while the others waited in the aspen and pine forest. Somi wanted to go with them but the boys thought it best that they go alone. If Mrs. Kee was upset with Somi and didn't want her to see Wai Chun Hing, the boys would still get to see him.

A couple of minutes after they went up to the house Hank was back.

"Hey!" Greg exclaimed. "What's with you? I thought Wai Chun Hing wanted to see you."

"So'd I, but he changed his mind. He took one look at Hip and asked if he was Chicano. When he found out he was, he ordered me out of the house. He said that he wanted to talk to Hip alone."

Time dragged endlessly. It must have been half an hour or more when Hip left the house and came across the narrow clearing to the place where his friends were waiting.

"How is he?" Somi asked.

"Better. They're planning to go to San Francisco on Monday morning."

"I'm going down to see him." Somi would have left but Hip stopped her. "It's no use," he said as gently as possible.

She stopped, hurt leaping to her eyes. "Doesn't he want to see me?"

"It's not that. His daughter doesn't want you to. As I left she followed me outside and asked if you were here. I guess she saw you guys. Anyway, she told me to tell you not to come, that she wouldn't let you see him. She's afraid you'll upset him or something."

Somi fought back the tears.

"Well, what did you find out?" Greg asked, to change the subject.

"And how come he sent me packing?" Hank Wendland broke in. "Did I do something to make him mad?"

"I haven't got a clue," Hipolita answered. "He asked me if I was a Christian and if the Powells were. Then he asked if I lived with them or had just come along, and a bunch of stuff like that. I asked why he wanted to know, but he wouldn't tell me."

"What about the newspaper story?" Greg put in impatiently. "What'd it have to say?"

"The paper was printed in Taiwan and the story was about that Generalissimo Chiang Kai-shek, or whatever his name was," Hip went on. "The guy the old fellow had a picture of."

Hip drew a long breath in his excitement. "It told about this general dying. There wasn't any date on the paper so I don't know when that was, but Wai Chun Hing knew about it, so it must've happened awhile ago. Anyway, the paper printed this guy's will. He said that he had confessed his sin and put his trust in Jesus Christ to save him, that he wanted a Christian funeral service and recommended that his followers read the Bible regularly, and one other book I don't remember the name of . . . "

"What'd he say about the stuff C. J. and Monte are selling?" Greg wanted to know.

Hip frowned. "He doesn't think they found it around here, that's for sure. But he didn't know where it could have come from unless it was stolen from the Palace Museum in Taipei, Taiwan. I guess there was a lot of stuff stolen from there a few years ago and nobody has seen anything of it since.

"He was looking for his pants—said he was going down to the old hotel with me to see the things, for sure, but Mrs. Kee said she wouldn't take him and for him to get back in bed."

"Did he think he'd know by looking at some of it?" Hank asked, glancing accusingly at Greg. That look was a silent reminder that Greg had been the one who had stopped them from getting a couple of pieces for Wai Chun Hing to examine.

"He said there were some pieces he would be able to recognize, he thought." They walked on for a moment or two in silence. "He said pictures would help, but he thought it was too late to get them. Then I told him about your Polaroid and he gave me a list of pieces to photograph. He said to get as close as you can to them and get the pictures back to him before the auction starts and he'll see if he can tell anything."

Greg brightened. "That's better. Maybe we can get to the bottom of this, after all."

"We'd better get that camera of yours and beat it over to the hotel so we can take our pictures and get them back to Wai Chun Hing before noon," Hip said.

At first Greg was going to ask Kim and Somi to stay at the motor home, but decided at the last minute not to. If he insisted, their folks might say they should all stick together and that would mean no auction sale and no pictures—which would ruin everything.

They stopped at the motor home long enough to pick up his Polaroid camera and flash attachment and tell his folks where they were going.

"Be sure to be home by dinner," Mrs. Powell told him.

He said they would and started up to Poor Boy's Folly. He didn't know when the visitors had begun arriving, but by the time they got to the ghost town the street was clogged with cars and pickups.

"Man," Greg said in tones little above a whisper, "this is really a blast. There's a bigger crowd here now than there was at the first auction."

Hip and Hank surveyed the cars critically. While they watched, several more vehicles drove by, looking for some place to park.

"We'd better get in and get those pictures," Hank muttered, "or there'll be so many people we won't even be able to get close to the tables."

Greg felt his heart hammer erratically as they entered the building. He blinked in the dim light and waited for his eyes to grow accustomed to the semi-darkness. For a moment he hesitated, hoping C. J. and Monte were not in the old hotel lobby. He had been praying that the two men would be gone—just for five minutes—long enough to get the pictures Wai Chun Hing suggested and split for the old man's place. For once he wasn't going to let curiosity trap him in the hotel. Not after what had happened in the last auction.

"Crowd around me," he whispered to his companions. "We've got to keep those dudes from seeing what I'm doing."

The kids moved over to one of the tables in a group and kept close around him while he focused on a hand-carved ivory ball, a little smaller than a tennis ball. It was an intricate piece of work with a ball within a ball—nine balls—carved from a single piece of ivory. Greg took the picture and for a brief instant the flash seemed to light up the entire room. Greg glanced quickly about, but neither Monte or C. J. seemed to notice. He breathed his relief and moved on.

The next item he was looking for was an Oriental junk, also carved of ivory. The little boat was small enough for a man to hold in the palm of his hand—three or four inches long, Wai Chun Hing had written—with the other dimensions to scale. There was no sign of it—in spite of the fact that they had covered three-fourths of the display.

He wasn't sure whether or not the next piece was on one of the tables. Wai Chun Hing had written 'one cloisonne vase in greens and gold—8 inches high.' Greg didn't know what cloisonne was, so he tried to find a vase of various shades of green and gold.

The chances were that Monte wouldn't have noticed him at all if Greg hadn't been so engrossed in finding the next item on the list that he began to move in the opposite direction of the crowd. Near the back of the lobby he found a vase he thought fit the description and took the picture. As the flash went off he felt a heavy hand clamp on his shoulder.

"You!" Monte snarled. "I thought I warned you about taking pictures the last time."

"I—I—" he stammered, trying in vain to wriggle free.

"Come in here!" Monte ordered in a taut whisper, jerking him toward the rear door. "All of you—if you don't want this kid to get hurt!"

"Run!" Greg hissed between clenched teeth. "Get out of here while you've got a chance!"

But he was too late. C. J. pressed close behind the others, crowding them through the rear door.

"Help!" Kevin shouted, his voice shrill. "Help!"

Monte cursed and drew back his hand to hit him but the door behind them opened and two or three men came out.

"What's going on here?" one of them demanded.

"We caught these kids trying to steal from us," C. J. said.

The spokesman didn't know Greg but he knew Hank Wendland. "How about it, Hank?" he asked.

"No way. Greg was just taking some pictures and these guys blew their cool."

"How about it?" another asked Greg.

For answer the boy showed him the print that he had stuffed in his pocket. He held it momentarily until the sunlight developed it.

"You can search us if you want to," Greg told the men. "We didn't take anything."

"Well—" C. J. and Monte were deeply disturbed, but tried to keep from showing it. "You have to be so careful with kids these days to keep 'em from stealin' you blind."

"I think you and your friends hadn't better come back inside, Hank," the man who knew him said. Deliberately he turned to C. J. and Monte. "And you two had better keep your hands off these kids, if you know what's good for you."

"What kind of men do you take us for, anyway?" C. J. demanded indignantly. "We're certainly not going to hurt any kids."

"Fine. Just see that you don't!"

Greg led his companions down the alley at a rapid pace. "Man, that was close!" he said when C. J. and Monte were back inside and no one was in sight along the alley. "If it hadn't been for that friend of yours, Hank, we'd have been in real trouble."

The kids went down the alley to the end of the row of empty buildings, crossed the road and headed into the woods in the direction of the motor home. They hadn't gone more than 40 or 50 paces when Monte appeared suddenly in front of them, a revolver in his hand.

"All right!" he said gruffly. "Stop right where you are!"

"You heard what Mike said," Hank told him. "You'll be in real trouble if you don't let us go."

"Your friend Mike's not going to know anything about this 'til the sale's over and we've split. Come on! And don't try anything funny! See! One more scream like you gave back there and it'll be the end of you!"

"Watch it, Kev," Greg ordered quietly.

"Now you're gettin' halfway smart."

Monte rushed the kids across the street and back to the alley, then herded them ahead of him to the old Oriental store building. He threw Greg a key and ordered him to unlock the padlock on the back door.

"Then open the door and give the key back. Understand?"

The older Powell boy did as he was told.

Monte got a flashlight from the bench in the back room, flicked it on and shoved the kids ahead of him down into the cellar, where he again had Greg open a padlock—this time on the trap door to the tunnel. Greg did as he was told, but not before noticing some torn pieces of foreign newspaper and others in English lying on the dank floor. One had the masthead of the paper published years ago in the mining town—*The Poor Boy's Gazette*. He stopped for a moment and was pondering the matter when Monte prodded him with his foot.

"Be quick about it!" he ordered.

"You can't do this!" Hank protested.

"Don't worry!" he said, laughing nastily. "We'll phone old Heskett before we catch our flight out of the country and tell him where you are. He ought to get you out in a couple of hours."

Greg was afraid someone would mention the cave that the tunnel led into, but no one did. No one, that is, except Monte.

"And one more thing!" he exclaimed before closing the trapdoor. "There was a little cave that led into the end of the tunnel, but don't bother trying to go back to it, thinking you can go back to the ruins of that old mansion. We knocked down some of the timbers and the tunnel is blocked—but good!"

With that he shut the door and snapped the padlock in place. His laughter carried down to the frightened kids crowded together in the tunnel.

16

The kids huddled together in the darkness of the tunnel for a minute or more, not daring to speak. Their breath came in short, thin stabs and sweat was clammy on their foreheads.

"What're we going to do?" Hank demanded at last.

"You heard C. J. and Monte!" Hip retorted. "The tunnel's blocked behind us and the trapdoor's padlocked." He tried to laugh but there was no humor in the shrill cackling sound that drifted over to Greg.

"All we can do is wait for them to phone Mr. Heskett," Hip continued.

"You should live so long!" Hank blurted, hysteria climbing in his voice. "Those dudes won't come back for us or phone anyone to tell where we are, either. We'll never get out of here!"

At that Somi began to cry softly.

"Watch it, Hank!" Greg countered sternly. His own heart was hammering and he felt an icy emptiness in the bottom of his stomach, but he couldn't let the others know that. If they panicked they would be in more serious trouble than they were already.

Someone had to stay cool and that someone was him. "We're locked in, but we're not going to stay here and wait to be found! We'll get out of here on our own!"

"And just how are we going to do that?" his new friend wanted to know.

144

"H-How about praying?" Kevin asked uncertainly.

"I should have thought of that myself," Greg said.

"Me, too," Hip murmured.

"A lot of good praying'll do," Hank retorted. "We're trapped down here. It'll take more than prayer to get us out of this mess."

Ignoring him, Greg asked Hip, Kim and Kevin to pray. When they had done so, he concluded the brief time of prayer by asking God to give them courage and wisdom to know what to do to get out of the tunnel.

"We should have done our praying before we got down here," Hank muttered.

For a time all was silent. Then Kim spoke up. "Think it'll do any good to yell?" she asked.

"Who's to hear us?" Hank Wendland wanted to know. "We're in a tunnel way down in the cellar of a building there's nobody in—or even near. We could yell for a thousand years and nobody'd hear us!"

"How about working on the trapdoor?" Hip asked. "There are six of us. If we'd all get under it and shove with everything we've got, we might be able to push it out."

Greg said it was worth a try, but in his heart he didn't think it would do any good. He had examined the trapdoor earlier. It was made of heavy oak and mounted in oak planking that was securely anchored in the floor. The builder hadn't wanted to take a chance of having the tunnel broken into if the trapdoor was discovered. Greg didn't think there was any way of getting it open.

And that proved to be the case. They shoved until their arms trembled, but it was no use. The hasp rattled noisily against the padlock, but nothing gave.

"See!" Hank exclaimed. "It's no use, I tell you! We're trapped! We're going to die down here!"

"Shut up!" Greg ordered sternly. "Nobody's going to die."

Somi started to whimper again and, although they said nothing, Greg was sure Kim and Kevin both felt like it.

"All right, wise guy!" Hank growled to Greg. "If you're so smart, how are we going to get out? Answer me that!"

At that moment Greg didn't know what they could do. It would have been easy for him to agree with his friend and sit down, yet something compelled him to go on.

"We can't do anything at this end," Kevin piped suddenly. "Why don't we go back and see if the tunnel is really blocked."

"It'll be blocked, all right," Hank complained.

"You've got a good idea, Kev," Greg said. "Come on, gang!"

They started up the narrow tunnel in the darkness, feeling the cold walls with their hands and advancing slowly, one hesitant, faltering step after another. Once or twice Greg stumbled and almost fell, but was able to catch himself.

"Hey, Greg!" Hip said, laughing nervously. "You forgot to turn on your flashlight."

They had traveled some 40 or 50 feet when they came to the place where the tunnel was blocked. They couldn't see it clearly, but Greg caught his toe on a rock and sprawled forward on the debris. For an instant he lay there, breathing heavily.

"What'd I tell you?" Hank demanded.

For a few moments silence gripped them. In the pitch blackness they could not see each other, but Greg knew that his own face was pallid, and that stark, unreasoning fear lurked in his eyes. He didn't think he had ever felt so helpless or so afraid. Yet he had to keep his head and keep trying to get the others out of the tunnel. For some reason he was the one they looked to for guidance.

He certainly didn't feel like a leader. He was as frightened as anyone else. Only someone had to keep the others calm.

"What do we do now?" Hank asked.

"Let's start trying to dig ourselves out," Greg said. The suggestion startled him. He hadn't even thought of it until the words came out.

Hank's laughter was hollow and scornful. "Are you out of your mind? Those guys have probably touched off a couple of sticks of dynamite in here. There'll be a hundred feet of rocks and dirt to go through."

"We don't know that," Greg countered. "Besides, there are six of us. We can move an awful lot of stuff if we get at it."

147

"Go ahead if you want to," Hank Wendland muttered. "I'm not goin' to waste my energy on anything so stupid."

"OK," Hip said, pushing past him and stopping to pick up a rock. "Just get out of the way so the rest of us can work."

They set to it mechanically, clawing their way through the dirt, rocks and half-rotted timbers. The area was so small only two or three could work at a time. They stayed at it until they were panting and out of breath, then they moved back and sprawled on the damp tunnel floor to rest while the others took over.

As they worked without any indication that they would be successful, despair tightened its grip on Greg. There was a deep weariness in his arms and legs and the fear in his heart took root and flourished. Had he been alone, he might have given up, but with the others there he couldn't.

He knew if he ever showed his lack of hope, Somi would go to pieces, and so would Hank, and possibly his younger brother. So, with a prayer for strength in his heart, he kept at it. Lift a rock and throw it back. Lift a rock, throw it back. Over and over and over—those same back-breaking motions. It was exhausting work, but as long as he kept at it there was little time to think.

Hank had moved aside at first, refusing to take his turn, but after a few minutes he joined forces with the others. Greg didn't know whether there was a little hope and faith flick-

ering within him after all or if he, too, felt that
he just had to do something to keep his mind
occupied.

Greg didn't know how long they had worked.
It may have been minutes, or an hour or two.
Time had seemed to stop its forward movement.
He had lost all track of it.

Then Hip cried out suddenly.

Greg looked up. "Eh?"

"Come over here!" There was an urgent tone
in his voice—so urgent Greg dropped the rock
he was moving and groped his way over to his
friend.

"What is it?" he asked.

"Feel!" He took Greg's hand and moved it
upward and to the right. "Feel anything?"

At first he couldn't be sure. Then it seemed
as though there was a faint movement of cool
air—so thin and light he marveled that Hip had
noticed it. In the pitch darkness he thought at
first that his friend might be breathing lightly
on his hand.

"Is that you?" he asked.

"Me?"

"Yeah, you. Were you blowing on my hand?"

"No way." Hip laughed again. This time with
relief. "My breath's not that cool!" He paused
briefly. "I think we're getting through! I've been
feeling that air for the last few minutes."

"What?" Hank demanded from where he was
working.

"Come over here and see for yourself," Greg said. "I believe Hip's right. There's cool air moving through this little hole."

Hank felt it and cried aloud—exultantly.

"We're goin' to make it! We'll get out of here yet!"

There was a prayer of thankfulness and gratitude in Greg's heart as he set to work.

"Thank You, Lord," Hip murmured.

"I don't think God had much to do with it," Hank said.

They had, indeed, broken through the debris that blocked the tunnel. In a few minutes they had moved enough rocks and dirt to allow them to crawl through to the freedom of the cave.

"I don't think they used dynamite on this," Hank observed as the last of the group wriggled through the opening to the other side. "If they had, it would have blocked a longer section than this."

"Maybe they just knocked down a few timbers," Greg said, "or they might have fallen in on their own. But I guess it doesn't matter. We're out now."

"If there isn't another cave-in," Hank said uneasily.

"Hey, quit that!" Hip told him as they gathered themselves in a line and started forward once more. "We're supposed to think positive."

They traveled forward as briskly as possible without a light. Now and then someone stumbled and fell but they all stopped and waited for him to get to his feet again. Finally they saw a faint streak of light at the end of the cave.

"We made it!" Greg said as he stepped out into the brilliant sunlight. "Thank You, God. Thank You!"

An awkward silence followed.

"What now?" Hank asked.

Greg hesitated. Ever since they had been locked in the tunnel they had concentrated on getting out. They hadn't thought about what to do to stop C. J. and Monte after they were free. Now he didn't know what to do.

"We could go down to the store and phone the sheriff," Kevin suggested.

"Mr. Heskett's closed," Hip replied. "I saw him at the auction. Besides, how do we know anyone would believe us? Those dudes would just lie about it."

"I suppose you're right," Greg answered. Then he felt the pictures in his shirt picket. "I know!" he exclaimed. "We can still go down and see Wai Chun Hing! He might be able to recognize the pictures I took."

They decided that Hank and Kevin would go back to the ghost town with the girls while Greg and Hip dashed to the home of Wai Chun Hing.

"Mrs. Kee'll never let you in," Hank exclaimed, grinning. "She'll take one look at you two—dirty as you are—and that'll be the end."

"She'll have to listen!" Greg said. "We're not going home and take a bath first. And we've got to have her father's help."

"Come to think of it," Kim said, "we look as bad as you do. What do you suppose people will say when they see us?"

"Nobody'd better see you 'til we get there!" Greg ordered. "And especially C. J. and Monte!"

"Yeah," Hip said. "We don't want to have to hunt you up again, after all that's happened so far today."

The two boys sped down the steep slope, crossed the road and plunged into the thick forest in the direction of Wai Chun Hing's house. When they got there the elderly man was out in the yard, leaning heavily on his cane. It was obvious that his arthritis was still bothering him. Hurriedly the boys told him everything that had happened and gave him the pictures. He squinted at them intently, holding them close to his faded eyes.

"I don't know," he said at last. "These pieces both look as though they could have come from the museum in Taiwan. I can't be sure. I suppose only an expert could be, but I can tell you this much. Those men are up to something illegal! They have to be stopped!" He raised his voice. "Leslie! Leslie!"

His daughter came to the door, irritation stamped on her features as she saw Hip and Greg. "What now?" she demanded.

"Get the car!"

"I will do no such thing!"

"Get the car, Daughter!" His voice carried a tone of authority. "I don't want to have to tell you again!"

"But—"

"Come on, boys," he said, hobbling toward the vehicle his daughter had rented. "Get in the back seat. I'll sit up front!"

"But Father!" she protested. In spite of her disapproval and hesitation, however, she did as she was told.

"Drive! Get up to the old hotel as quick as you can!"

"And then?"

"Let the boys and me out and go to the store or some rancher's—any place to get to a phone. Call the sheriff and get him over here as quick as you can!"

"What are you going to do?" she asked.

"Never you mind what I'm going to do! You get the sheriff!"

She stopped in front of the hotel, still protesting to her father that he was not well enough to be out.

"I don't care whether I'm well enough or not!" he snapped.

With that, he got out of the car and joined Hip and Greg on the sidewalk. "All right, boys," he said, hobbling forward with grim determination. "Let's go inside!"

17

At the door of the old hotel Wai Chun Hing stopped and stared after his daughter until the car disappeared from view. "She's a good girl," he muttered. "Just has to be straightened out once in awhile." Then he motioned for Greg to open the door.

As they went inside Hank and Kevin and the two girls came out of the shadows between two buildings and joined the tense trio. The auctioneer was holding a hand-carved piece of jade and was about to start taking bids on it when Wai Chun Hing hobbled forward.

"Wait!" he cried. His voice quavered but he spoke loudly enough to stop the sale. Every eye in the place was fixed on him and his youthful companions. The instant C. J. and Monte saw the kids their faces went ashen. Greg expected them to bolt for the rear door, but they did not. Their surprise was so great they seemed unable to move.

"I want this auction stopped until the authenticity of these pieces has been determined by an impartial expert," the Oriental exclaimed, "and the ownership of them has been determined!"

C. J. stepped forward quickly. "That's already been done!" he said. "And there's no question about ownership! We bought the property these pieces were found on, fair and square. We hold legal title to them."

That seemed to stop Wai Chun Hing. He blinked uncertainly and turned his watery gaze away.

"Go on with the sale," C. J. told the auctioneer.

But the stubby, balding stranger did not seem anxious to do so. "The old man's made a charge that we're selling stolen property," he said. "That's serious for me and anyone who buys it!" His eyes narrowed. "And it's even more serious for you. I'm not going on until I know that everything's clear."

"But I assume full responsibility."

The auctioneer turned to Monte. "Is this stuff stolen or not?"

"I've phoned the sheriff," Wai Chun Hing said loudly. "He'll be here any minute."

There was a surprised stir in the crowd, the sound of voices expressing concern.

"Good!" the auctioneer replied. "This sale will be stopped until the sheriff arrives and says it's all right to continue."

"You can't do that!" C. J. blustered.

"I just did." The auctioneer rapped the podium sharply with his gavel.

C. J. and Monte glanced significantly toward the door and began to inch in that direction. They were almost there when Greg saw what was happening.

"Hey!" he cried. "Stop those guys! They kidnapped us and locked us up!"

At the sound of Greg's voice C. J. and Monte burst through the rear door on their way to their car. But they were not without company. Mike, Hank's dad's friend, recognized Greg from the photo incident earlier in the day and sensed that he was telling the truth. He dashed after the men and several others followed suit.

They reached the would-be fugitives just as C. J. was beginning to back hurriedly out of the parking place.

"Oh no you don't!" Mike cried, jerking open the car door and wrenching C. J. from behind the wheel. "I think you'd better stick around to talk to the sheriff!"

The car, still in gear, backed across the alley and slammed into a huge pine tree, crumpling a fender. A couple of the other men grabbed Monte while he was scrambling to get under the steering wheel and drive away.

"You'd better stay here, too. I don't think the sheriff would like it if you leave without talking to him."

"We haven't done anything," C. J. protested.

"Then you don't have anything to worry about," Mike retorted.

Under the grilling of the sheriff and the county attorney, C. J. and Monte confessed to having bought several crates of Oriental art objects that had been stolen from the Palace Museum in Taipei several years before. They hadn't known how to dispose of their purchase safely until they heard about the first auction at Poor Boy's Folly. They had come up and looked the place over, then bought several buildings and pretended to make the find in one of them.

They also bought several boxes of imitation Oriental antiques from Hong Kong and mixed them with the authentic stuff to be advertised for the auction. They had taken the pieces out of their original Chinese newspaper packing and substituted old copies of the *Poor Boy's Gazette* to increase the likelihood that they would get away with their scheme. Bribing a so-called expert in Oriental art to certify that everything being sold was authentic was the final touch in trying to fool the buyers with the faked pieces.

"And," Wai Chun Hing told the boys when he and his daughter were sitting in the Powell motor home, "they would have gotten away with it if it hadn't been for you kids."

"You were the one who put a stop to it," Greg said.

"After you got suspicious and came to me." He was about to say more but his daughter broke in.

"I think it is time for us to leave now, Father. You are very tired."

"I ought to know when I'm tired or not," he retorted indignantly.

Her cheeks colored and she fell silent.

"I've got some things to talk over with my friends."

She acted as though she was about to get to her feet. "Would you like me to leave?"

"No, that won't be necessary. You can stay as long as you don't butt in when I'm talking."

Mrs. Powell excused herself to make some tea. That didn't seem to bother Wai Chun Hing.

"You're the one I really want to talk to," he told George Powell. "I've been doing a lot of thinking since the boys brought me that clipping of the Generalissimo—the one that must have been wrapped around one of those art pieces that was stolen in Taipei. . . . You know what that clipping was about, don't you?"

"Not exactly."

"It was what the Generalissimo had to say about being a Christian and following the Bible. Your family is the only one I've met who does that."

"We don't do it as well as we should, I'm afraid," Mr. Powell told him. "But what does that have to do with—"

"Don't get in such a hurry. I'm coming to that. I'm not going to be able to stay here alone any longer," he said. "I'm going to have to live with my daughter."

"I'm glad you're coming to your senses, Father," Mrs. Kee broke in.

The old man warned her to silence with a glance. "And I'm not going to be able to take Somi with me."

The girl, who had been sitting quietly in a corner until that instant, caught her breath sharply.

"I can't manage it alone and Leslie doesn't want Somi in her home, so it's no use even trying to think about keeping her."

Mrs. Kee's cheeks darkened with embarrassment. "I just don't have room," she replied lamely.

"Nonsense! You don't want her. Why not be honest? And it would not be good for Somi to live there when my daughter feels the way she does. That is what I want to talk to you about."

The elderly Oriental man leaned forward. "You would teach Somi about the Bible if she lived with you, wouldn't you? The same as Madame Chiang Kai-shek taught the Generalissimo?"

"Of course," George said.

"I know you would treat her well," Wai Chun Hing went on. "I have questioned my good friend Hipolita Rodriquez about the way you treat him. He says it is the same as though his skin was as light as yours."

"Why wouldn't we?" Greg broke in. "Hip's my best friend."

"I have decided to ask that you take her and raise her as your own daughter, Mr. Powell." He paused for a moment. "Would you grant a tired old man so great a favor?"

"We would love to have her. We've talked with Miss Grainger, the social worker, about it. But she says that Somi's aunt wants her with a Thai family. She's coming in to Denver tonight to help work things out."

The elderly man brushed the objection aside.

"She wants only to be sure that the child will be well treated. I will talk to her. I will fix it."

"But, Father!" his daughter protested.

"Silence! This I must do for my Somi, who has brought so much joy to my own heart. I just want to see that she has what is best for her."

He turned toward the girl. "You would like that? No?"

Somi's small, oval face lighted. "I think I would like that, Grandfather." She flew to his arms and kissed him.

"And you listen well when your new father teaches you about the Generalissimo's Bible. It *must* be the way of true happiness or so great a

Bernard Palmer

man as our Generalissimo would have seen the error in it."

Greg's heart filled as he looked over at Somi and realized that she would be living with them from that time on as their new sister. How God had answered their prayers!

Hank, who was sitting beside him, squirmed. Greg glanced his direction and their eyes met. There was a questioning look on Hank's face that let the older Powell boy know that at last Hank's defenses were down and his heart was seeking peace and security and the assurance of salvation.

The Powells were going to be in Poor Boy's Folly for several more weeks. Before they left, he was sure that his new friend would confess his sin and receive Christ as his Saviour.

Mrs. Powell came in and kissed Somi on top of the head. "Somi," she said softly, "would you and your sister like to help me serve the tea?"

A quick smile flashed through the tears. "Certainly, Mom." She paused momentarily. "I can call you Mom, can't I?"

"I'd feel badly if you called me anything else."

Kim and Somi went out into the kitchen with Mrs. Powell. As they did so, Greg saw that all three were crying, but they were tears of joy. He understood. His own eyes were misty.